STONE RAID

A STONE COLD THRILLER

J. D. WESTON

WESTON MEDIA

STONE RAID

CHAPTER ONE

"We're in position, Fingers," said Dynamite into his hands-free comms. He pulled his scarf back up to cover his face and checked the darkness around them. "Give us a countdown."

"Copy that," replied Fingers, tapping away on the keyboard. "Perimeter security is going down in three, two-"

"Hold on, hold on," said Dynamite. "Give us a bit longer than three bleeding seconds, will you? How long is our window?"

"When I kill the security system, you'll have twelve-seconds to get inside and close the window before the backup power kicks in, and the systems boot up."

"What happens if we don't have the window closed within twelve-seconds, Fingers?" asked Lola. She stood beside dynamite beneath a large window.

"Well," replied Fingers, "for a start, it's going to get awfully loud, and I imagine the place will be lit up like a Christmas tree. Then, of course, the automatic locks will kick in, steel intruder barriers will drop down over the doors and windows, and that lovely manicured lawn that you two just crawled across will likely be a car park for the dozens of police that will no doubt arrive in a matter of seconds. Not to mention, their helicopter will need somewhere to land. You two, of course, will be none the wiser as you'll both be shut inside waiting to be caught like a right old pair of donuts."

"You paint a pretty picture, Fingers," said Dynamite.

"It's a pretty diamond, Dynamite," replied Fingers. "From what *I* hear anyway."

"You heard right."

"Right, let's get our act together, boys," said Lola. "Fingers, give us ten seconds."

"Copy that."

His fingers danced across the keyboard, entering a string of code into the command line interface of the security hub, and then stopped, poised above the enter button.

"You ready?" he asked.

Dynamite lifted the jimmy bar to the window lock and worked the pointed end into the small gap between the window and the frame.

He took a breath and looked at his partner, who nodded in silent reply.

"Go," said Dynamite.

Fingers began his count.

"Ten."

"Lola, get ready to climb up," said Dynamite.

"Seven."

Lola readied her boot on the smooth surface of the wall and reached up to the window, ready to grab onto the frame as soon as it opened.

"Three."

"Our lives will be very different in about fifteen minutes' time," said Dynamite.

"One."

Dynamite heaved back. Wood splintered loudly in the quiet

night as he forced the window open. Lola was up on the ledge before it had opened fully, then she launched herself inside. She immediately turned and helped Dynamite inside, who fell to the floor then bounced back up to force the window back into place.

The tiny copper connections touched.

"Perimeter security is back online," said Fingers. "It's all on you guys now. You've got approximately one hundred and eighty seconds until the infrared fires up, which means that you have one hundred and sixty seconds before I kill the security again."

Lola was already running her hands along the glass cabinet in the centre of the room. Even in the darkness, the golf ball-sized diamond reflected tiny fragments of light.

"Hello, sweetheart," she spoke softly.

Dynamite stepped over to her. "Don't just look at it, Lola," he said. "One-thirty and counting."

Lola fumbled beneath the cabinet, pulling at wires. She flicked on her head torch.

"One-twenty."

Lola closed her eyes and began pulling a tiny wire from its connector.

"Just pull it out, Lola," said Dynamite.

"Hold on," she replied. She reached further into the cabinet. "Aha." Her tongue slithered out between her lips in concentration.

"Don't give me that bleeding *aha* business, Lola," said Dynamite. "One hundred seconds."

"Dynamite, just keep cool."

"Yeah, we'll both be bleeding keeping cool in an eight-by-five cell for about twenty years."

Lola tugged at something and brought out a little black box.

"What's that?" asked Dynamite.

"It's a keep alive," said Lola. "It's attached to the alarm system and the backup power. It sends a tiny voltage to the sensors, so even if the power to the security system goes down, the alarm won't. My guess is that it's attached to an independent network that goes directly to the police."

"Your guess?" said Dynamite. "We don't have time for a guess. He checked his watch. "We have ninety seconds to get the diamond and get out. It was your bleeding job to do a recce."

"Eighty-seven," corrected fingers.

"If I pull this wire, there'll be police all over this place in a matter of minutes. And yes it was my job to do the recce. But you know what, Dynamite? When I came here on a tour, for some reason, the guide wouldn't let me look underneath the cabinet and refused to answer my questions about the alarm wiring."

"Fingers, are you scanning the police frequency?" asked Dynamite.

There was no answer.

"Fingers?" said Lola.

"What happens if we smash the glass?" asked Dynamite.

"Smash the glass? Dynamite, this is *not* a smash and grab. We are a pair of highly-skilled professionals. It's bad enough that you broke the window. Talk about leaving a calling card. No wonder they call you-"

"Okay, okay," said Dynamite, holding his hands up defensively. "So what do you want to do? Leave *without* it?"

Lola looked down at the diamond.

"It's awful pretty, isn't it?" she said.

"Second only to you, babes," said Dynamite.

Lola continued to stare at the diamond, mesmerised by the perfect sparkles.

"We have thirty-five seconds, Lola."

Lola looked up at Dynamite from where she crouched

beside the cabinet. "Get ready to run like you've never run before."

She pulled the wires. There was silence.

"Silent alarm?" asked Dynamite.

Lola lowered the panel beneath the cabinet then stood cradling the velvet cushion with the rock sat on top. Dynamite grabbed the diamond and stuffed it into his pocket.

"Fingers, come back."

No response.

Lola replaced the velvet cushion, and then returned the wires to their connections.

"Fifteen seconds," said Dynamite. "Fingers, we're ready. Shut it down."

No response.

"Bugger this," said Dynamite. He yanked the window open, which immediately sounded the shrill alarm that pierced their night like a banshee. Flashing red lights fixed above the doors and windows began to spin and sent the dark room into a frenzy of beams.

They both dove through the window together and landed in a pile on the gravel pathway that wound around the old building. It acted as a border to the immaculate lawns, which were now fully illuminated by giant spotlights on the rooftop that covered every inch of the grass around the house.

The steel intruder barriers slammed down into place behind them.

"Go," said Dynamite, half-dragging Lola along. "We need to move."

Lola ran alongside him towards the tree line at the far side of the lawn. Her heart thumped with adrenaline. They'd done it; they had the diamond. It had taken a few weeks of planning, and everyone said that it couldn't be done, but they'd finally got it.

Dynamite burst through the trees in front of her into the small clearing where they'd left Fingers in the back of the van.

"Fingers, start the engine," shouted Dynamite as he ran. "Fingers?"

Lola could just make out the shape of the van in the darkness. She saw Dynamite come to a sudden stop. Lola stopped beside him.

"What?" she asked.

Then, as if they'd just run into a football stadium, lights hit them from all around. Five sets of car headlights, all on full, all turned on together and pointed directly at where Lola and Dynamite stood.

"Shit," said Dynamite.

A man in a long, black leather jacket stepped out of the shadows and into the centre of the mock arena, his huge frame silhouetted by the dazzling car headlights. Without a second's hesitation, he pulled a handgun from his jacket, raised it and fired once into Dynamite's face.

Without stopping, he lowered the gun, remorseless, as Dynamite's body folded to the ground in an undignified heap.

Lola stood stiff, too scared to move or even to wipe Dynamite's spattered blood from her face and lips.

The man in the jacket turned to her and spoke with a cold, deep voice that seemed to rumble like thunder.

"Hello, sweetheart."

CHAPTER TWO

For Harvey Stone, being back in London was less than ideal. But the fact of the matter was that he was laying low, and laying low meant finding somewhere unfamiliar, somewhere he'd never been before, and keeping out of sight. He'd spent eighty-nine days staying inside his bedsit. On the occasions that he had to venture out, he tried to blend in. He'd enjoyed a few early morning runs before the sun rose. But he tried to limit them to once or twice a week.

It was a far cry from his preferred lifestyle. Although Harvey typically led a basic life, far from lavish, his main issue now was that he had nothing to occupy his mind. His home in France had taken much of his time. It was a small farmhouse and each day he'd set about completing the minor jobs that needed doing. He'd replaced the roof tiles, sanded and painted the wooden window frames and doors, and cleared the gutters ready for winter. But then his life had been turned upside down. He felt it was wise to stay away for a few months.

It was the thought of returning to his house, walking on the beach and riding his motorcycle along the winding lanes of the southern French coast that kept him going, and staying away for a few months was the sacrifice.

He was beginning to get stir crazy. It would be time to return home soon, just one more day. He could, of course, return any time he wished and deal with whatever came his way. But he'd set the three-month target, he'd made the plan, and breaking the plan for the sake of boredom and one more day didn't sit well with Harvey.

That's how mistakes happen.

Harvey sprinted the final stretch of forest and tore out of the trees into the small back streets of South London. Harvey was an East London man through and through. But laying low in East London was too dangerous. He was too well known by the wrong people. South London had enough migrants and cultural diversity for him to become just another person in the crowd.

He walked the short distance to his bedsit, a small room with an attached bathroom in a terraced house. It offered a view of the houses on the street behind and a dull, grey sky.

The entrance to the old Victorian house was up three stone steps and through a wide front door into a hallway. His room was directly in front of the stairs on the first-floor landing. When he'd agreed on the rates with the landlord, he'd had the choice of the basement room, the first floor or the second floor. Harvey had selected the first floor because the peephole gave him a direct view of the stairs and the length of the hallway. Plus, if the worst happened, he could always get out of the sash window and become quickly lost in the maze of gardens.

The room had a single bed and an old, tired-looking, wooden wardrobe. An ageing lamp with a yellowed, frilly shade stood on top of an even older bedside table. The room was slightly larger than a prison cell with just enough floor space for Harvey to do push-ups and sit-ups. An old TV sat on top of the wardrobe, but Harvey hadn't turned it on in the three months he'd been there.

In some ways, the time had been good for him to reassess his life, make decisions, and to reflect on his past. In other ways, it had been a prison sentence.

Harvey climbed the stairs to his landing quietly and respectfully of the other tenants. He hadn't even reached the top stair when he noticed the shiny new lock on his door. A few steps later, he saw his bag sitting on the floor outside.

There was no point in trying his key in the new lock. He picked up his bag and checked his belongings. A small secret pocket at the back held his few personal possessions. Nothing was missing.

A younger and less mature Harvey might have kicked in his landlord's door and said farewell. But the older and much more tired Harvey took the hint. The landlord had eyed Harvey with suspicion from the off. Harvey had paid in full for three months with fresh banknotes in a bank seal from a small stash of cash he kept for emergencies. The landlord had also asked questions that Harvey had preferred not to answer. Instead, he'd topped up the bundle with more banknotes; one hundred pounds per question, plus an extra two hundred to avoid providing a copy of his ID.

Harvey's total words spoken during the entire process of viewing the room had been only six, while returning the old man's feeble prompts at conversation with cold stares.

He swung his pack onto his shoulder and dropped his key on the floor by the door. It was useless anyway.

The landlord occupied the room beside the front door. As Harvey stepped off the stairs, he sensed rather than heard the man standing behind the door, peering through the peephole, dressed in the same old grey cardigan and slippers that he always wore.

Harvey opened the front door, stepped outside and breathed the fresh air. It was summertime, the air was cool but not cold, and Harvey felt good to be out of the house. The decision had been made for him, and although the following night would be uncertain, he was grateful.

Freedom could be measured in so many different ways, he thought. For some, freedom meant being released from a term under Her Majesty's pleasure. Or it might mean financial freedom. For Harvey, right there and then, stood on the doorstep of the old Victorian house he'd holed up in for nearly three months, freedom meant going home.

But the mantra that Julios had etched into Harvey's mind as a young man seemed to burn at the thought of breaking a plan so unnecessarily. One more night. He could do that. He could find somewhere to get his head down.

One more night. Then the long trip back to France.

CHAPTER THREE

"What do you mean you let her go?" asked Charlie Bond. "You're six foot four and had a dozen blokes with you."

Rupert stood from his desk. His chair scraped across the floor. "Don't talk to me like that, Charlie. I've told you before, I won't stand for it."

"What do you want me to say, Ru? Never mind, come sit down, and have a cup of tea?" He sighed with frustration. "Did you get it, or not?"

Rupert stepped across the floor of their shared office. His brogues sounded solid on the hardwood. He poured himself a whiskey from their crystal decanter and sank it back in one hit.

"You need to give me a little more credit, Charlie," he said, as the liquid fired through his throat.

"So you got it then?" asked Charlie. His voice was serious but a creeping smile betrayed his tone.

"You need to keep the boys low for a while, Charlie," said Rupert. "The old bill turned up within minutes of the bells."

"You said they would," replied Charlie. "Anything I need to be concerned about?"

"Glasgow George had to kill her fella."

"He had to?"

"Yeah," said Rupert. "We've got his body down at Doctor Feelmore's morgue."

"And what was the particular reason he felt it necessary to kill him?" said Charlie. "I mean, other than his passion for blood."

"I told him to. We needed to get her attention."

"Pour me one of those, will you?" asked Charlie.

Rupert poured another glass and refilled his own.

"So you got her attention, and then what?"

"The old bill turned up," said Rupert. "Just like I told you." He set the crystal-cut glass on Charlie's desk, which was the twin of Rupert's own.

"And did you all stop and *wait* for the old bill, Rupert?" said Charlie. "This is like getting blood from a stone."

"Well, if you want to be in the know-"

"I know, I know," said Charlie. "I should have been involved. But some of us had other things to attend to, didn't we? We can't all go gallivanting around in the countryside late at night."

Rupert smiled at his brother and sank his drink once more.

"We're rich," he said. His smile broadened into a grin showing his perfect teeth.

"I know we're rich, bro."

"No mate, you don't understand," said Rupert. "We're even richer."

"So you did get it. I wondered when you were going to drop the bombshell and put me out of my misery."

"You need to see it to believe it," said Rupert. "I've never seen anything like it. It's almost..." Rupert searched for the right word to describe the diamond.

"Almost what?"

The words found Rupert as another scotch burned its way to his stomach. "Otherworldly," he said finally.

"Otherworldly?" said Charlie. "Is it from another planet?"

"It's beautiful."

"You look like you just saw your first naked woman, Ru. Get a grip and don't get attached to it. We're selling it."

"Yeah, but you should see it, Charlie. And feel it."

"I'd love to see it and feel it, Ru. So where is it?"

"Somewhere safe."

"Somewhere safe?" said Charlie. "Where?"

"I had Smokey take care of it. He's trustworthy."

"Smokey the Jew?" said Charlie, leaning forward in his chair. "You've got to be having a laugh with me."

"He's sound, Charlie," said Rupert. "What would *you* have me do? Bring it back here?"

"Rupert, you could have given it to anyone. In fact, I told you to get it straight to Dirty Thanos down at the kebab shop. He owes us a favour or three. He could have kept it hidden in a slab of meat or something. What the bloody hell did you give it to Smokey for?"

"Because, Charlie," replied Rupert, as he made his way back to his desk with a freshly poured scotch. "Dirty Thanos is exactly as his name suggests, a dirty kebab shop owner. He only knows two things, how to make a kebab and how to butcher a carcass." Rupert took a sip of his drink. "Now, if we were getting rid of something, such as a body or something we never wanted to see again, I'd have taken it to either Dirty Thanos, so he could cut it up into tiny pieces and feed it to the Albanians, or Doctor Feelmore down at the funeral parlour, so he could incinerate it. But as it happens, Charlie, this is the one thing we don't want to have cut up into tiny bits and it's definitely not something I would suggest incinerating. It's a priceless diamond the size of bloody golf ball. So I gave it to Smokey the Jew to keep at his house, which I might add, due to his family's light-fingered habits and passion for rare and expensive art, is like a bleeding fortress."

"Who else knows Smokey has it?" asked Charlie.

"The only people that know Smokey has it is me, you and Smokey."

"And what happens if he does a runner? He could leave the bloody country with it. Actually, no sorry, let me rephrase that, he could *buy* a bloody country with it, then go live there while we suck it up here in London in the freezing bloody cold."

"You talk crap sometimes, Charlie," said Rupert, leaning back and putting his feet on the desk. He ran a soft tissue across the front of his shoe. "You know what your problem is?"

"Enlighten me, oh wise one."

"See, Charlie, you've always been the same. You're lucky to have me around, you know?"

"Is that right?"

"Yeah, it is. You just don't have the vision, Charles. You can't see past next week. It's all now, now, now. But what about tomorrow, eh? What about when all this comes crashing down and the clubs are shut? Booze is getting more expensive. I'm sometimes embarrassed how much we charge for a glass of Chablis."

"And what is it that gives you this all-seeing eye then, Rupert?" said Charlie. "What is it that sets you apart from the rest of us mere mortals?"

"I can read, Charlie," said Rupert.

"We can all read."

"Yeah, but I like to read the things that matter. I don't just stare at the pretty pictures of pretty ladies, do I?"

Charlie continued to stare at his twin brother as he sat, looking smug in his fine leather chair. "Go on, then," he said. "What have you read?"

"I thought you'd never ask," replied Rupert. He put his feet down to the floor, straightened his cuffs, and smoothed the back of his head with his hands. "We're going to be double rich, bruv."

"What are you on about?" asked Charlie.

"That diamond, Charlie," said Rupert, leaning forward with his elbows on his knees, identical to his brother. "It's a bit like you."

"Good looking, you mean?"

"It's worth a small fortune."

"Yeah, we established that. That's why we-"

"But," said Rupert, raising his index finger to quieten Charlie, "it's worth a fucking mint when it's with its twin brother."

CHAPTER FOUR

"Morning, Melody," said Reg Tenant as he entered his office.

Melody had already been sat at her desk working on her laptop for an hour. She didn't look up. "Hey, Reg," she replied, barely distracted from her work. "Did you bring coffee?"

"You're empty?" asked Reg. "Do you want to take a walk? We can grab a cup, and I have some news you need to hear. It might be best to discuss it off-premise."

"Sounds ominous," said Melody.

"Ominous? No," said Reg. "Dangerous? Yes."

Melody glanced away from her screen.

Reg smiled back at her.

"You're going to love this one. It's got your name written all over it."

Melody scrambled a few more words onto the keyboard, hit save then shut the lid of her laptop.

"What was that?" asked Reg.

"Just a report I'm finishing off."

"The Jackson case?"

Melody nodded but couldn't meet his eye.

It had been close to three months since their boss, Jackson, had tried to frame Melody's fiancé for murder. Jackson had been killed when his elaborately prepared grand finale backfired, and they had all escaped. Harvey hadn't been seen or heard from since. In the end, the wrong man wasn't found guilty, but Melody's life was still turned upside down. She'd moved from their farmhouse in France back to London, and buried her head in work to get through it.

"Why don't you let me finish that off?" said Reg. "Come on. I'll brief you while we walk."

Melody sighed and stood. She followed Reg out of the office, and they waited by the elevator.

Reg checked around him then began to talk.

"Have you ever heard of the Demonios Gemelos?"

"Demonios Gemelos," repeated Melody. She thought for a few moments. "That's devil twins in Spanish?"

"Well, it means twin demons to be precise, but yeah, it's the same thing."

"No," said Melody. "I can't say I have."

"Well, you'd better learn what you can because your foreseeable future revolves around them."

The doors to the lift opened and Reg, ever the gentleman, ushered Melody inside first. Another man occupied the lift, so the pair remained silent until he got out on the next floor. Melody waited for the doors to close fully before she spoke.

"Are you going to give me a clue?" she asked.

"A clue? Okay," said Reg. "Put it this way, if that engagement ring that Harvey bought you had one of them in it, you'd be dragging your hand across the floor."

"It's a diamond?" asked Melody. She subconsciously glanced down at her engagement ring. She hadn't been able to bring herself to remove it.

The elevator stopped on the ground floor and the pair walked through the security barriers, flashed their badges and stepped out of the Secret Intelligence Services building onto the footpath of London's Southbank.

Melody usually felt an immediate tension release each time she left the building, but she was deep in thought.

"Twins?"

"It's a pair," said Reg. "They aren't the largest diamonds ever found, but together, they're almost up there with the Crown Jewels."

"What's with the name?" asked Melody. "Twin demons. I mean, it's quite a negative name considering what they're worth."

"Rumour has it that whoever holds them both at the same time comes to an unexpected and unfortunate end."

"Folklore?"

"Just a series of unexplained mysterious deaths, I imagine, mixed with a large dose of coincidence. They were dug up by the Dutch in South Africa during the days of the British Empire. Some English guy had a fight with some Dutch guy and won. So, as the legend goes, he stole them. From there, they were exported to England as a gift to Queen Victoria. No doubt a ploy to win her favour."

"But?" asked Melody, sensing the direction of the tale.

"The ship sank."

"Funny that," said Melody.

"The opportunist captain killed the diamond thief when he knew they were going down and jumped ship with them. He made it as far as Europe."

"Then what happened?"

"He made it in a lifeboat to the shores of Portugal, evaded capture and wound up in France with a few of his shipmates.

They, in turn, robbed him of his quarry and turned themselves into the British Army in France seeking safe passage back to England."

"I have a feeling they didn't survive?" said Melody.

"Two of them did actually," said Reg. "There were three of them, but neither could agree on who looked after the diamonds, so one of them stole them one night."

"Don't tell me," said Melody.

"They caught him, and he was killed," continued Reg, "and the remaining two kept one each."

"And because they didn't carry them both together, they both survived?"

"So the legend goes, Melody."

"Coincidence?"

"That's my opinion," said Reg. "I'm a tech guy remember. Things are black and white."

"You sound like Harvey," said Melody quietly.

"I might have stolen a line or two from him." Reg grinned.

They strolled along London's south embankment at a slow pace. Reg left the silence for Melody. He knew she would be devising a list of questions.

"So the diamonds," began Melody, "was that what the robbery in South London was about? The one I read about in the paper?"

"Yes it was," said Reg. "Very sharp." But he offered no further insight.

"And they are considered unlucky when together?"

"Yes, apparently."

"So my guess is that if someone robbed the first diamond," said Melody, "a diamond like that might be worth a small fortune. But both of them together?"

"Who knows?" said Reg. "They haven't been in the same

country since nineteen forty-eight when the second diamond was stolen."

"Nineteen forty-eight?" said Melody. "And they're both in the UK now?"

Reg nodded.

"The current owner, a Dutch gentleman, as a matter of fact, came forward and was putting one up for private auction. He said his family acquired it shortly after the Second World War. It was being kept at a private house out in the country somewhere."

"That's where it was robbed from?"

"Yeah, crazy, isn't it?" said Reg. "The old guy who owns the house is an Earl of something who agreed on the use of his safe room, as the Dutch guy didn't trust the greed of the English."

"It wasn't a very safe room though, was it?"

"The room had steel slam doors and windows, a direct connection to the local police who were notified the second the security system connection went down, and laser motion sensors. All of which were powered by UPS backup power supplies."

"Sounds serious. What else does he have in there?" asked Melody.

"We don't know. But we do know that they didn't take anything else and they only just got out in time. The slam doors and windows were down. Whoever stole it took all the precautions they could to get in, but the secondary circuit beneath the display cabinet had been pulled. It was shoddy work, Melody."

"How would the thieves have known about the security systems?"

"Same way they always do," replied Reg. "Research, visits, and talking to the right people, I guess."

"It's open to the *public*?" said Melody, incredulous. "What were they thinking?"

"It's a National Trust building, Tudor, I think, maybe earlier."

"So how did they get in?" asked Melody. "I mean, I'm guessing they got in without raising the alarm?"

"Yeah. I took a look at the system. It's definitely the work of a team, minimum two, probably three or four."

"Three or four," said Melody thoughtfully. "One to break in, someone light on their toes with knowledge of security and nerves of steel."

"Or just plain greedy," said Reg.

"They'd need someone with tech skills," said Melody. "Someone like you, Reg. What were you doing last night?"

Reg laughed. "I have an alibi. I was having dinner with Jess in the local curry house."

"A likely story," said Melody, toying with her friend. "The other two may have included a driver and some muscle."

"I'd agree," said Reg. "We can't be sure of the exact skill set of the team, but something this big couldn't be done alone."

"So they got in without raising the alarm but triggered it when they took the diamond?"

"The circuitry beneath the cabinet looked as if they just ripped the cables out."

"Not very pro," said Melody.

"Nope."

"You think someone came along and disturbed them?"

"The guards were all doped. Three of them were found face down in the control room."

"So what happens when the circuitry is broken?" asked Melody. "Where does the alert go?"

"The police station gets an instant alarm. It's a special arrangement the owner of the house has with the local unit."

"Would they have known that?" asked Melody. "The thieves, I mean, would they have known about the direct link?"

"They had a false alarm last week," said Reg. "Some guy leaned on the case and set it off."

"My guess is that he was number three or four in the clan."

"Copy that," said Reg. "Some guy with a false name, fake ID, he even had fake prints. Police arrived on the scene in under three minutes. The thieves would have been timing it and drew their own conclusions."

"So I presume the thieves still have the diamond?" asked Melody.

"Yep," said Reg. He held the door of the coffee shop open for Melody.

"And can I presume that you now think they will target its evil twin brother?"

"Demonios Gemelos," said Reg with a smile.

"But it's a diamond robbery case. Why are we dealing with that?" asked Melody, under her breath as she joined the small queue. "It's not exactly secret intelligence, is it?"

"We're not dealing with it," replied Reg with a smile. "*You* are." He continued to watch the barista as she darted around behind the counter, foaming the milk for one drink while hot water ran through the grinds into two other cups.

"*Me?*" said Melody. "On my own?"

"Special orders," said Reg. He eventually turned to face her. "You've been selected, Melody."

"Me? But why me?" she asked.

"You were an excellent operative. Plus, you had success with the jade buddha case. If you remember, most of that operation was accredited to you."

They were called to the counter, and Reg placed the order. A flat white for Melody and a tall hazelnut latte for himself.

"It's a great opportunity," said Reg. "A real chance to get back in the game. You *are* going to take it, aren't you?"

"Of course I'll take it," said Melody. "Do we know where the other demon twin is kept?"

Reg smiled at the cashier as he received his change, and they moved to the collection area of the counter.

"You're going to like this, Melody. It's in the Natural History Museum."

CHAPTER FIVE

"It's not much, Fingers, but at least it's out of the cold," said Lola. She dropped another Daily Express into the fire they had created in the old disused warehouse. She bent down to the bundle of unsold papers and grabbed another one.

"How long did you say we're going to stay here?" asked Fingers. He looked around the room, which seemed to be an old office when the warehouse was habited, and saw nothing but gloomy shadows. Strange noises issued from the larger space outside, the creaks of old beams and groans of walls, and ceilings cooling after a day of rare British sun.

"As long as it takes, Fingers," replied Lola. "I still can't believe-"

"Hey, Lola, don't go there," said Fingers. "Come on, we're still in this, and we won't get through it unless we-"

"Unless we what, Fingers?" snapped Lola. "Forget about him? Is that what you were going to say?"

"No, I-"

"Well, I can't forget about him. He meant too much to me to just forget."

"I'm not talking about forgetting Dynamite, Lola. God, he

was my mate. But you know what? We can still remember him. Remember how he used to be able to make you laugh at just about anything?"

"Yeah, he did," said Lola. Her voice was quiet and thick with suppressed emotion.

"He was always like that, you know?" said Fingers. "He always had this way of making people smile, especially at the most inappropriate times. This one time we were in school and the teacher, Mr Day his name was, kept picking me out to answer his questions. So I'd have to stand and answer him in front of the whole class. Dynamite was sat behind me, and I can't remember what he was saying now, but all I could hear was Dynamite's voice, and all I could do was try not to laugh. Mr Day, as you can imagine, was slowly getting more and more frustrated with me. I couldn't even look at him. I just stared at the floor. My face went bright red, and my body was shaking with laughter until finally he exploded, Mr Day that is. He went into an absolute rage, which was even more hilarious because he was bald with these two tufts of hair above his ears, and when he got mad his entire bald head creased up."

"So," said Lola, "what happened?"

"I couldn't hold it any longer. I burst out laughing and, of course, the rest of the kids all fell about too. Mr Day was apocalyptic. He began screaming at everyone, and you know what?"

"What?"

"The only two people in that room that weren't laughing was Mr Day and Dynamite. I don't know how he did it, but Dynamite just sat there straight-faced, looking at me like I was completely nuts and didn't understand what was happening, which was even worse because I took one look at him and it sparked me off again."

"Always the joker, eh?"

"He was a legend, Lola. An absolute legend."

A moment's peace followed as the pair were each lost in their own thoughts of Dynamite. Lola broke the silence by tossing another newspaper into the small fire.

"Shame we don't have a little bottle of brandy to toast him, eh?" said Fingers.

"We will, Fingers," said Lola. "We will."

"Have you thought about what that bloke said at all?"

"I can't do it," replied Lola. "How could I? He just killed..." Her voice broke off.

"But you know if you don't do it, you'll be hiding like this for a long time? You're going to need a bigger stack of papers, Lola."

"I could disappear," she offered. But immediately, she knew the idea was weak and impossible.

"Disappear, yeah?" said Fingers. "Where would you go? You know it's just a matter of time before they track you down."

"Yeah, but honestly, how powerful do you think these people are?" asked Lola.

"The Bond brothers?" asked Fingers. "Only the most powerful villains this side of London, Lola. They've got their fingers in a lot of little pies, and if there's a cash business this side of the Thames, you can bet your arse they're involved some-how. They own most of the clubs, they run the security for the ones they don't own, and the rest of the firms all fall under their protection. Trust me, I know them well."

Lola gave him a grave stare across the fire. The shadows ran deep beneath his eyes.

"Mark my words, Lola," said Fingers. "Doing the job is the only way out of this."

"It's a betrayal, Fingers," replied Lola. "Imagine what Dyna-mite would have said? Besides, it was only ever about that one diamond."

"Dynamite isn't here, Lola. I know it's hard to hear. But you know what? You need to survive. You need to live and you need to remember him, whatever it takes. Giving up and having the Bond brothers on your case for the rest of your life isn't going to solve anything, and it isn't going to give you much chance of remembering Dynamite."

"How, Fingers?" said Lola. "I've got two options. One is certain death. The other is almost certainly prison time."

"You don't reckon it's possible at all then?"

"Listen, Fingers, you've seen the place, right? You know the security. If jobs were like dinners, what we did last night was cook sausage and mash potato. Robbing a post office would be like making a sandwich. But robbing the other diamond would be like cooking a lobster thermidor with one hand and knocking up a crème brûlée with the other. Do you know what I'm trying to say?"

"I've never known you to back away from a job before, that's all, Lola," said Fingers.

"I'm not backing away. I'm laying it on the table, Fingers. Whichever way you look at it, my life is over."

Fingers suddenly flinched. His eyes widened and turned slowly to listen at the door. Lola questioned him with a look. Fingers returned the question by mouthing two words.

"Someone's coming."

CHAPTER SIX

The plastic tarp crinkled loudly as Harvey ran his hand along it. It hadn't been moved since he was last there. Old dusty boxes full of meaningless junk, a few battered oil drums that had been used as rubbish bins, and some heavy machinery with a thick coat of grease across their cast iron housings stood against the far end of the warehouse as if they had been forgotten. Perhaps the removal firm had placed them there to be removed last but had never returned to collect them. The machinery looked outdated and useless. The boxes were filled with ancient printouts on dot matrix paper. Whatever was printed on them had long since been relevant to anybody.

On the cold and dirty concrete floor beside the boxes, and stacked neatly in comparison to the other random items, were twenty or thirty large bundles of newspapers. They were probably dumped there by a lazy paperboy with better things to do than walk the streets. There was a pile of old timber, which was likely scrap from when the chainlink fence had been erected around the property. All the doors were boarded up.

The warehouse itself was over a hundred meters long with a wall of offices along one side and huge, arched windows on the other. The ceiling stood high above Harvey's head, maybe thirty or forty meters, and the occasional pigeon made himself known with a shake of feathers and some verbal warnings.

The daylight was fading, but any romantic imaginings of times gone by or sentiment had been lost on the place. It seemed as if life itself inside the old factory had been lost to the shadows for decades, despite the enormous windows.

Harvey stayed close to the wall. A faint glimmer of flickering orange shone briefly from an office at the far end of the warehouse.

A fire?

Maybe a homeless person?

They would be no trouble, thought Harvey, as long as they kept to themselves.

Harvey stepped into the first office space in the long row that ran along the far wall. It was a small space with the same high ceiling as the factory floor and similar large windows. Harvey imagined the office once belonged to the manager of whatever production line used to be immediately outside the room. The same for the rest of the offices. Each manager might have been responsible for a particular production phase.

Harvey had no knowledge of such things. He just imagined.

Long shadows began to reach across the warehouse space outside as the sun dipped low enough to find the floor through the arched glass. The light cut through the dust in the air, forming identical golden beams that grew brighter and weaker as clouds moved across the sky.

Harvey sat in the corner with his rucksack beside him. It wasn't so bad for one night. He'd stayed in worse places for longer. At least he had a roof over his head. During his walk along the canal outside, Harvey had seen the thunderheads moving in from the west, patiently waiting like an ancient army stood at the edge of a city before the command to strike unleashed hell.

As if on cue, a scatter of rain danced across the roof high above, and the golden beams of light faded to shadow, leaving nothing but darkness in their wake.

A scuffle of feet on the concrete floor outside caught Harvey's ear. He listened harder. People. But they were moving away. He glanced around the corner.

It was two men.

Harvey moved towards the doorway but remained inside the small office. He clung to the shadows and followed their movements across the vast open space outside.

A lifetime of finding people, watching them and following them had taught Harvey a great deal about body language. The two men weren't casually taking shelter from the rain; they were creeping towards the room at the end of the warehouse. The room with the fire.

The two men each wore a short bomber jacket, jeans and boots. Harvey noted their appearance; they weren't homeless. Maybe it was a gang meet. They looked like heavies. They walked with the confidence of men who carried weapons, were used to hurting people, and who stayed at arm's length of the law.

Harvey knew the type all too well.

What Harvey found odd was that a deserted warehouse should see so many visitors in one evening.

Harvey didn't believe in coincidence.

In Harvey's mind, either things were, or they weren't. They were black, or they were white. Idealism might be good for businessmen. But in reality, ifs and buts created cracks in plans, doubts in minds and failed missions.

Failed missions often resulted in death.

The angle of Harvey's view became too narrow to track the

men, so he waited a full one minute, which was his standard practice before making any moves. The full minute had been a lesson from his mentor, Julios. If anyone was listening for him or waiting to jump him, most men would grow impatient long before a full minute passed. It also allowed him time to formulate some kind of plan and question his motives.

He could and perhaps should stay sitting in the corner of his empty office on the hard floor and listen to whatever was happening. It was none of his business anyway.

Or he could stick to the shadows and watch from a distance. It was the closest he'd been to anything exciting for three months.

Lightning flashed outside. It lit the windows and left a photographic image of the empty warehouse bathed momentarily in unnatural light on Harvey's retinas.

The lightning passed, and his vision faded back to the darkness. Rain drummed on the roof like the well-timed footsteps of a thousand soldiers marching to war.

The warehouse appeared darker than before as if the thunderclouds had banished the golden sun and cast long, dark fingers across the eyes of the world.

Harvey peered from the office. The men had disappeared.

Finally, a crack of thunder announced the arrival of the storm. It was followed quickly by another flash of sheet lightning that once more lit the open space, while a rumble of thunder rolled across the sky.

Small drops of water had found a leak in the roof and landed on the floor close to where Harvey stood with an increasing rhythm.

Suddenly, a girl screamed somewhere at the far end of the rumble.

Battle had commenced.

The screaming continued. Harvey pictured the girl in a

room much like the one in which he was stood. She would be cornered and frightened with no exit.

One of the men shouted for her to shut up. His rough, baritone voice seemed to carry across the floor and below the girl's screams, which sung through the eaves of the huge ceiling.

Harvey stepped outside.

CHAPTER SEVEN

Rupert put his phone down on the desk and opened an internet browser on his computer.

"Who was that, Ru?" said Charlie, looking up from his own screen.

"Glasgow George," replied Rupert. He ran a search for a satellite map of South London and began zooming in.

"Are you going to tell me what he said?" asked Charlie. "Or are we playing guessing games now?"

"He put a GPS tag on the girl. He's found her and has sent Mad Bob and Cannon Bill to keep an eye on them."

"Oh, so not important news then? Was you actually *going* to tell me?"

"Charlie, when I receive a piece of information as important as this, I like to digest it. I like to think of all the possible outcomes and then articulate a reasoned summary of A, what might happen, B, what I'd like to happen, and C, what the plan might be if indeed circumstances lean towards the non-preferred option A."

"You do talk crap, Rupert," said Charlie. "They found the girl, so there's only one option."

Rupert looked across at his brother who span his chair to gaze out of the floor-to-ceiling windows covering the wall behind their desks.

"And that is?" asked Rupert.

"Grab her, give her a slap, and make sure she does exactly what she's supposed to do."

Rupert shook his head. "And that is why I prefer to absorb the information before it's allowed to be put through your simple mind only to have answers spat out like a wood chipper, Charlie."

"Where is she?"

"In some factory somewhere down by the canal. I'm just looking it up now."

"So she hasn't gone home then?"

"No, obviously she hasn't."

"So why do you think she hasn't gone home then?" said Charlie. "She's planning on doing a runner, and if she does a runner, you can bet your arse she's planning on an anonymous call to the police with a little tip-off about who has got the diamond."

"Charlie, you're a muppet sometimes," said Rupert. "She knows that if she goes home, we'll know where she lives." He turned back to his screen and found the factory that Glasgow had described.

"Care to explain?" asked Charlie, tapping away on his phone and letting the insult wash over him. The two brothers enjoyed the banter, but they only tolerated the insults from each other. Nobody else dared to talk to them in anything less than a respectful manner.

"She's scared, mate. She's just seen her bloke get his face blown off, and then a dozen big blokes, namely Glasgow George and his mob, gave her two choices. Neither are favourable for her future."

"She's scared?"

"Yeah, she's scared. The only way out of this is for her to get the second diamond for us. If we go in there and give her a slap, she's even more likely to do a runner, which means in turn that we'll have to find her, kill her and finish the job ourselves. So that means we'll either be less rich than we had planned or we'll have to risk bringing some other thief in to do the job for us. That's a bit risky, mate. We're not robbing cash vans here. This is serious stuff, Charlie. It needs to be handled delicately."

Charlie was silent. He put his phone in his pocket and carried on looking out of the window at the big black clouds that had begun to roll in. Small specs of rain dotted the outside of the glass and lights across the city started to blink on as the sunlight was quenched.

"Charlie?" said Rupert.

"Yes, brother," replied Charlie, in the mock tones of a well-to-do manservant.

"Do you realise that if we do get this other diamond, that's it for me, I'm out?"

"What do you mean you're out?"

"Charlie, we're talking millions here, mate."

"We already have millions. We'll just be richer," said Charlie. "No, nothing will change. The business needs you. It needs us both."

"No, you don't get it, do you? We won't need the business. We won't need to sit up here and make sure people are doing their jobs. We won't need to make sure none of the men are helping themselves or taking liberties. And we won't need to cock about with backhanders, which, by the way, are getting way out of control now. Do you realise how much we paid last month just to stop the old bill giving us grief?"

Charlie looked across at his brother, but let him continue his rant.

"Fifty grand, Charlie," said Rupert. "Fifty bleeding grand in some copper's skyrocket, just for him to turn a blind eye."

"It's been happening for years, Ru. I wouldn't let it worry you. We make that back in a night."

"Yes, I know we make it back in a night, Charlie. But my point is that we wouldn't have to, would we? No, we wouldn't. We'll be sitting on a beach in the perpetual sunshine, someplace classy with a cocktail in one hand and a tart on each knee fighting over which one of them is going to rub the suncream on my chest."

"Is that right?" said Charlie, smiling at the picture his brother had painted.

"Yes, it is right, and all we have to do, dear brother, is keep our nuts firmly screwed on, keep our beady eyes on the beady little bird, and wait for her to deliver us from evil, as it were."

"Deliver us from evil, Ru?"

"Yes, Charlie. With what little Lola is going to give us, and what we've already taken off her, I intend to live within the remits of the law. I'd like to walk down the street one day, preferably in the sunshine, and not have to look over my shoulder, and not have a carload of Mad Bobs and Glasgow Georges following me. I'm tired of it all, Charlie. We could have a great life. Think about it."

"And all we have to do is...What was it? Keep our heads screwed on and keep our beady little eyes on the beady little bird? I'm pretty sure I can handle that."

"That's it, bro," said Rupert. "Think of the sun, the sand, the semi-naked women." He stopped. "*Charlie?*"

"Yes, bro."

"What have you done?"

"What do you mean what have I done? I haven't done anything."

"You just agreed with me," said Rupert. "You *never* agree

with me that easily. Who did you just text? I saw you on your phone."

"Ah well, you know," said Charlie. "The sun and...What was it? The semi-naked women. I'm game for it. Look at this rain, eh. I'd love a bit of sunshine right now."

"Charlie?"

Charlie fell silent.

"Charlie, *who* did you text a minute ago?"

"No-one special."

"*Charlie?*" Rupert raised his eyebrows. He'd caught the bit between his teeth. "You just text Mad Bob, didn't you?"

Charlie didn't reply.

"You *did*, didn't you? You bloody *idiot*. You told him to give her a slap."

"I might have," said Charlie. A grin began to ease itself across his face. "But in my defence that was *before* you gave me all the talk about beaches, sun and semi-naked women."

"What have you done, you idiot? If he hurts her and messes this up, *I'll* kill him."

Rupert jumped up from his chair, grabbed his phone and hit Mad Bob on speed dial. He listened intently to the dial tone until the call was eventually answered.

CHAPTER EIGHT

"Oh finally," said Melody, sitting back from her laptop. She was sat on the guest side of Reg's large desk. Behind Reg was a view over the River Thames and Vauxhall Bridge. Melody enjoyed watching London from Reg's office. The day had been particularly nice with a rich blue sky that seemed even to brighten the river of endless, murky, brown water.

By evening, however, the blue sky had been pushed to one side to make way for an approaching storm. The soft hues of blue had been replaced with an impenetrable layer of grey. The clouds quenched the distant parts of the horizon with imposing shadow and banished the city into darkness.

"Finally *what?*" asked Reg, engrossed in his work.

"I've finally managed to get hold of the technical drawings and CAD files."

"For what?"

"The museum," said Melody with an accomplished smile. "They don't make it easy, but it's all out there ready for the taking."

"So why do you need the CAD files?" asked Reg. "You know you can walk right in, don't you? You're a member of secret intelligence. I'm sure a few phone calls could arrange it."

"*I* know that and *you* know that. But the thieves don't have our credibility, so they can't just walk right in, and for me to understand how they're going to do it, I need to think like them."

Melody sat back in her chair.

"The thieves will need to go through the same research as I have, with a little help from the tech guys, which means that I can study the same drawings and files to work out how *I* would rob the museum."

She smiled across the desk at her friend, who remained focused on his work.

"What's the matter? I thought you'd be proud of me."

"Well done, Melody," replied Reg. "Sorry, I am proud. But to be honest, I have no doubt whatsoever that you can stop them. I wouldn't have asked you if I thought otherwise."

"Hey, Reg?"

"Yes?" he replied, his eyes still on his computer screen.

"Reg?"

He glanced at her.

"Are you happy?" asked Melody. "With the job, I mean. You miss the tech stuff, don't you? The nitty gritty."

Reg sighed and closed his eyes.

"I guess I do," said Reg. He pushed his keyboard away and leaned on the desktop. "I see Jess and the guys down in the operations room, and I see you getting small wins, and yeah, I totally miss the challenge. All I seem to do is write reports. If I need research done, I have a team to do it for me, and even watching them is frustrating, Melody. Is it wrong to think that..."

"To think what, Reg?" asked Melody.

Reg sighed. "To think that I can still do it better and faster?"

Melody set her laptop down on the desk and crossed her legs. "You want to talk about it?"

"What's to say?" replied Reg. "I just remember the times we used to work for Frank. We pretty much had free reign to do what we wanted, *and* we achieved excellent results."

"You feel constrained here?"

"A little, yeah," said Reg. "I'm ready for a change. I used to love seeing a problem, and in my mind, I'd match a technology to the problem then I'd go away and create something." He met Melody's eyes. "All I create here is reports for someone upstairs to read and then file."

"You're not solving crime," said Melody.

"I'm not solving anything, Melody. I'm barely using my brain, and yes, it's great to see you being given a case and to see you immerse yourself in it, and believe me, all I want to do is jump on that case with you, but I can't. I'm tied to this chair with so much red tape."

"Why don't you help me?" Melody asked.

"How can I? I have to finish this report, then I have to pull up performance stats, after that, I have the hugely unsatisfying task of creating a resource forecast. A *resource forecast,* Melody. A forecast that tells my superiors what resources I will need for the forthcoming year."

Melody held his gaze but pitied him. She could see he was frustrated.

"How the *hell* am I supposed to know how busy we'll be in a year's time?" Reg continued. "*I* don't know how many people I'll need or what technology we'll need. The technology we'll be using in twelve months might be totally different. And to top it off, it should be *me* creating the technology. That's what I'm *good* at. That's what I *enjoy.*"

"So, why are you doing this, Reg?"

He let his head fall into his hands. "Oh, I don't know. It seemed like the right career move, you know? The one that would take me to new levels."

"And has it?" asked Melody.

"New levels of boredom is where it's taken me."

"Boredom?"

"Well," said Reg, with a sheepish grin, "mostly."

"Reg," began Melody, "I've known you a long time, right?"

"Yeah."

"And we're good friends?"

"I think so," Reg confirmed.

"Since you've had this job, you've had a gun put to your head, you've been held hostage on a cliff face, and you've been tied to a tree waiting to be boiled alive."

"Rough, isn't it?" said Reg.

"The reports are just the end of a job, Reg. The truth is, and I say this as a friend, that maybe you're not the type of guy that enjoys the wild rides of an active case. You're always in your element at a computer, close to the action, but not in it. I can't remember how many times you've saved my butt from the comfort of your chair. There's no shame in doing what you're good at, Reg, not when you're as good as you at doing it."

"What are you saying?" asked Reg. "That I'm weak?"

Melody laughed at the comment. "No, Reg. You're one of the strongest men I know." She tapped her temple indicating his mental abilities. "I just think maybe you should dip your toe into the tech research side of things again. When is the next report due?"

Reg shrugged.

"Five days maybe?" he said.

"Okay, come help me work the diamond case. I'd say they'll hit the museum in less than five days anyway," said Melody. "Nobody is going to want to hang onto the dreaded Demonios Gemelos for too long."

Reg let his head hang low, and leaned his elbows on his knees. He looked up at her with a sheepish grin.

"Come on," urged Melody. "It'll be like the old days."

"You mean I can sit in a van with a laptop, while you go and risk your life?"

Melody's smile broadened, it was clear that Reg was up for the challenge.

"With you in my ear to keep me company, Reggie," she said, "it'll be an absolute pleasure."

CHAPTER NINE

"Evening all," said Mad Bob, stepping into the room. "Well this is *cosy*, isn't it? All we need is a few steaks and sausages and we've got ourselves a right little barbecue."

Lola backed up against the wall. The arched window above her did little to light the room, but the fire threw flashes of orange light. It was enough for Lola to see that the man's face looked like it had been chewed by a dog. He was large framed and moved with confidence, but his shape was nothing compared to the monster that stepped into the room behind him.

"What do you want?" asked Lola.

"What I want is for you to *shut up* and *listen*, sweetheart." He stared down at her as if to emphasise the point. "When I ask you a question, you can take that as a prompt for you to talk. But if I do not ask you a question, the best thing for you to do is keep that dirty little trap of yours shut." He glared at Fingers who stood close by Lola, keeping the fire between them and the two men.

"Now," he continued, "do you remember me?"

The pair nodded.

"Do you know who I am?" he asked. "I don't think there was time last night to make a proper introduction."

The pair shook their heads.

"You was one of the men that shot our friend," said Lola.

"Okay, we're making progress. But sadly, I didn't pull the trigger. Do you know who I work for?"

"No," said Lola, a little too quickly.

"No?" said the man. "Would you like to hazard a guess?"

A flash of lightning lit the room and his face. He looked like pure evil. His face was more scar tissue than skin. He grinned when he saw Lola's eyes widen in horror.

"Pretty, ain't I?" he said, his voice deep and grumbling.

Lola didn't reply.

"Let's start from the beginning, shall we?" he continued. "My name is Mad Bob. I wasn't christened Mad Bob, but my friends decided to call me that from an early age and it kind of just stuck, you know?"

Lola nodded.

"Do you know why they called me that?"

Lola didn't reply. Fingers stared at the floor.

"No?" he said. Then he raised his voice. "Right, let's get one thing straight, it seems I have to explain the fundamentals of basic human interaction. When I ask you a question, you answer. You speak loud enough for me to hear and clear enough for me to understand. When I don't ask you a question, you keep your mouth shut. But while you are holding them pretty little lips together, Lola LaRoux, you will listen to *every* word I say. You will make it your sole mission during the longevity of our conversation to ensure that every little word issued from my lips, every little detail whether spoken or insinuated, is understood. Carefully place it at the front of your grey matter, ready for you to call upon at any given moment, because, and I cannot stress this point enough, if I ask you to recall a detail, no matter how small, and you fail, then that is likely to upset my friend here and me."

He stopped and glared at Lola and Fingers who were listening intently.

"So, let's make it easy then, shall we? Do you remember playing a game when you were younger called Simon Says?"

Lola nodded.

Mad Bob stared back at her in disbelief.

"I don't believe it," he said. "I have just explained the fundamentals of basic human interaction, less than thirty seconds ago, and yet she still-"

"Yes," said Lola, growing tired of his voice. "Yes, I understand Simon Says."

"Good." Mad Bob turned to Fingers and raised his eyebrows, a gesture that, if it weren't for the firelight, Fingers wouldn't have seen.

"Yeah," said Fingers. "I remember."

"Excellent," continued Mad Bob. "We are making progress, or as my old man used to say, we are cooking with gas. Are we not? Now, are you both ready to play Mad Bob Says? It's similar to Simon Says, but with a slight variation."

"What's the variation?" asked Lola.

"Here we go," said Mad Bob. "I like it. We're interacting. The variation of Mad Bob Says to Simon Says is quite simple, Lola. Just as in the game of Simon Says, when I give an instruction, which is preceded by the words, Mad Bob Says, you are obliged to fulfil the request. But the variation is that, unlike in the game of Simon Says, whereby failing to fulfil your obligation merely results in you being out of the game, in the game of *Mad Bob Says*, failure to fulfil an obligation results in the breaking of bones. Your bones."

Mad Bob let the first variation to the rules of the game sink in before speaking again.

"The second difference between Simon Says and Mad Bob Says is this. In the game of Simon Says, you might get three lives before you are out. I think the rules vary from game to game. But when I was a child, we had three chances, and then we were out. However, this is the important bit. This is one of those bits of information I spoke of, which you need to stick in the front of your grey matter, darling. In the game of Mad Bob says you will only get one life. One attempt at fulfilling your obligation. Failure to do so will result, as I before mentioned, in the breaking of your bones. Every single one of them. One by one. Bone by crunching bone."

Another silence hung in the air.

"Now, shall we begin?" Mad Bob asked.

Lola didn't reply.

"Good girl," said Mad Bob. "She's sharper than she looks this one. *Mad Bob says* shall we begin?"

"Yes," said Lola.

"Yes," said Fingers.

"Good," continued Mad Bob. "Now, *Mad Bob says*, do you know why they call me Mad Bob? There's a nice easy one to start you off."

"Because you're mad?" said Fingers. "Ruthless?"

"Ruthless," said Mad Bob. "I like it. Yes. Although I am quite sane, some people tend to lean towards me being a bit of a psycho. Perhaps it's due to a combination of my lack of empathy, an unwillingness to recognise the needs and feelings of others, and an ability to inflict incredible amounts of pain onto another human being." Mad Bob gave his own statement some thought. "What do you think?" he asked.

Both Lola and Fingers remained silent.

"*Good*," said Mad Bob. "You're learning the rules. Now, *Mad Bob says*, are you having fun?"

Lola and Fingers glanced at each other then back at Mad Bob.

"No," said Lola.

"No," repeated Fingers.

"Good," said Mad Bob. He pointed a huge fat index finger at them both. "Because this is not supposed to be fun. This is supposed to be an exercise in ensuring that you fully understand the consequences of cocking me about and failing to fulfil your obligations."

Mad Bob stood straight again and cleared his throat.

"Now," he continued, "standing behind me in the shadows is my friend Cannon Bill, but you can call him Mr Cannon. He likes that. It appeals to one of the basic needs that Maslow set out as a framework for a human to feel part of society."

Lola looked past Mad Bob into the shadows but saw no-one.

"Why don't you say hello, Mr Cannon?"

Mr Cannon didn't reply.

"He's a man of few words," said Mad Bob. "Lola, why don't you throw some more of those newspapers on the fire? See if we can't light the room up a little."

Lola didn't move.

"Okay," said Mad Bob. "*Mad Bob says*, feed the fire, Lola."

Lola bent and pulled two more newspapers from the pile. She rolled them up and tossed them into the dying flames. The paper landed on the burning embers, shrivelled, then succumbed to the heat in a show of flames. The room flickered a bright orange haze, casting a Mad-Bob-shaped shadow onto the wall behind him.

A man stepped into the room.

Mad Bob sensed the movement.

"Ah, here he is. Mr Cannon. I knew he wouldn't be too far away."

He turned to face his friend, but instead he was met with an uppercut that rocked the big man's jaw and sent him crashing to the floor like a felled tree.

CHAPTER TEN

It took a few moments for Harvey to bind the big man's hands with his own bootlaces and take his weapon, which was a Glock. Harvey removed the magazine, made sure the chamber was empty, and tossed the gun on the fire. He pocketed the magazine and the man's phone.

Two terrified-looking faces stared at him from across the room.

"You've nothing to be frightened of," said Harvey. He stood over the man on the floor, waiting for him to come around.

"Who are you?" asked the girl.

"What's his name?" asked Harvey, ignoring the question.

"That's Mad Bob," said the small-framed man who stood beside the girl, "and that outside is Cannon Bill."

"*Mad Bob and Cannon Bill?*" repeated Harvey.

"Yeah, that's all we know," said the girl. She gave her friend a sideways glance.

Harvey dragged the man closer to the fire and rolled him onto his front.

"What are you going to do with him?" asked the girl. "Are you going to kill him?"

Harvey ignored her and stepped from the room into the darkness. He found Cannon Bill where he'd left him, dragged the huge man back across the concrete floor into the room, and dumped him down beside Mad Bob.

"Make yourself useful," Harvey said to the pair. "Take them newspapers apart and screw the pages up tight."

"These newspapers?" asked the man, pointing to the only pile of newspapers in the room.

Harvey gave him a look and then continued to arrange Mad Bob and Cannon Bill so they sat upright back to back.

"What's your name, son?" said Harvey to the man.

"I'm, erm, Fingers," he replied.

"Fingers?"

"Yes, that's what they call me, my friends, that is."

"Okay, Fingers," said Harvey. "Give me your belt."

"My belt?" said Fingers. "What do you-?"

The girl suddenly jumped into action. She stripped him of his belt then walked across to Harvey, who had sat Mad Bob and Cannon Bill back to back. She wrapped it around the two men's necks, fastening it tight with a snatch of her wrist.

She stepped back and admired her handy-work.

"What's your name?" asked Harvey.

"Lola," she replied. "Lola LaRoux."

"You've done that before?"

"I've seen movies," she said. "Why else would you want his belt?"

"You two are in trouble?" asked Harvey.

"Yes," said Fingers.

"No," countered Lola. "It's nothing we can't handle."

"I'll leave you two to it then," said Harvey, and made to leave the room.

"No, wait," said Lola, a little over anxious.

Harvey stopped but didn't turn.

"We might be in a *little* trouble."

"That's what I thought," said Harvey. "Good luck with that."

"What?" cried Lola. "You mean you're just going to leave these two here tied up?"

"Do you want me to untie them?"

"Well, no, but-"

"I didn't think so." Harvey left the room.

"But what's your name?" she asked after him.

Harvey didn't reply.

"We can pay you," said Lola, clearly clutching at reasons for Harvey to stay.

Again, Harvey stopped but didn't turn around. "What makes you think I need your money?"

"Why else would you be here?" said Lola. "It's an abandoned warehouse."

"It's raining," replied Harvey. "It's got a roof."

"You don't strike me as the type of man that minds getting wet."

Harvey didn't reply.

"You also don't strike me as the type of man who minds getting his hands dirty."

Harvey heard Lola step closer. She stood half in and half out of the doorway. The left side of her body glowed orange from the firelight, the right side awash in shadow.

"What was the point in helping us if you aren't going to finish the job?"

"I don't like bullies," said Harvey.

"So what was the point of having us screw up the newspapers?"

"Stuff the paper down their shirts, cover them with that fire-lighter and light a match."

"That's barbaric," said Fingers. He squeezed passed Lola and stepped out into the open warehouse.

"Why not just spray their clothes?" asked Lola.

"Paper ignites quicker and burns for longer than fabric. You'll do more damage."

"Who *are* you?" asked Lola again. "You're what, an expert in burning people alive?"

Harvey turned to face them. They stood side by side, like two children asking their older brother for help against a bully.

"I've dealt with men like that all my life," said Harvey. "They all have their weaknesses; you just need to find it. Fire is always a good place to start. We have a primal fear of fire. It'll break even the hardest of men."

"You've burned someone alive?" asked Fingers.

"You ask a lot of questions. Maybe that's why you're both in trouble," said Harvey. "You want my advice? Do what I said, then get out of here. Go find someplace else. Start over."

"That was the plan," said Lola. "But they'll find us. They have more resources than we know about. Besides, do we want to spend the rest of our lives looking over our shoulders?" She glanced at Fingers, who shook his head.

"So what did you do?" asked Harvey. "Men like that don't normally go after someone without good reason. My guess is that those two clowns work for someone else, someone with money and power. The type of man that employs people like your mates in there would need a strong reason to go after a girl and..." Harvey looked at Fingers, searching for the right word to describe him. "You," he finished.

"We haven't done anything wrong," said Lola. "They want us to do a job."

Fingers nudged Lola as if to shut her up. She glared at him and continued to talk.

"They want us to do a robbery," Lola finished.

"What are you robbing?" asked Harvey.

"A diamond."

"A diamond? Singular?"

Lola nodded.

"It's a big diamond then?" asked Harvey.

"Biggest I ever saw," said Lola.

"So you're thieves then," said Harvey. It wasn't a question, it was a statement.

"They work for the Bond Brothers," said Fingers. "They said they'd kill us both if we don't do the job."

"The Bond Brothers?" said Harvey. "Never heard of them. And you definitely can't run?"

Lola shook her head.

"What makes you think they'd actually kill you?" asked Harvey. "I mean, at a guess, I'd say that Mad Bob and Cannon Bill were sent to rough you up, to make sure you do the job. Am I right?"

Lola nodded.

"And where is the job?" asked Harvey.

"So you'll help us?" asked Lola. "You're *interested*?" Her voice perked up at the thought of help.

"Professional interest," he replied. "But I don't do robberies. You're on your own." Harvey turned away again

"*Wait*," said Lola.

Harvey stopped.

"You asked what makes us think they'd actually kill us."

"Yeah I did," replied Harvey.

"They shot our friend," said Lola. "Last night. I was there."

Harvey didn't reply.

"I was stood beside him. They shot him in the face." Lola's voice broke off as she finished the sentence. "Please, we need help. If not for the robbery, at least help us with these guys? Look at what they did."

Lola pulled up her sleeve and showed Harvey a wrist tag.

"Do you know what this is?" she asked.

Harvey nodded. "That's what you get when you're released from prison on parole, so the parole officer can keep tabs on you. It's GPS, right?"

"If I go home wearing this, they'll know where I live and my family..." Her voice trailed off.

"Was it Bill or Bob that shot him?" asked Harvey. "Your friend."

"Neither," Fingers said, taking over the chat from Lola, who was crying into her hands. "Some other guy, but just as big."

"They run this part of town?" asked Harvey. "The Bond Brothers?"

There was a small silence as Fingers clearly recalled the event. "Yeah," he replied.

Harvey digested the information. He'd seen many firms being run by all types of men. Some were hard, some were rich, and once they reached a certain level of power, they rarely got their own hands dirty.

"Fingers, do me a favour, will you?"

"What?" replied Fingers. "What do you need?"

"Stuff all that paper down Cannon's shirt."

Lola looked up from her hands as Fingers tentatively slipped past her and back into the smaller room.

"What?" she asked. "You're going to-"

"I'm going to get these clowns off your back. You can stay if you want. But I'd suggest you get out of London sharp, find some way of getting that thing off your wrist, and forget about your friend."

Harvey took six long steps to the room and entered in time

to see Fingers step away from Cannon Bill, who had begun to stir.

"You're awake," said Harvey. He reached out, took hold of Fingers' belt, and sliced it with his knife to separate the two men. Then he dragged Mad Bob away by his feet and sat him against the wall. Mad Bob stared up at him in silence, but his look said all he needed to say.

Harvey returned his attention to Cannon Bill.

"Where can I find your boss?" asked Harvey.

Cannon Bill remained silent.

Harvey landed the sole of his boot onto Bill's face, sending him back onto the concrete floor. He struggled with his bound hands but eventually managed to sit back up. Blood trickled from his nose and the pages of rolled up newspaper stuck out from his shirt like a cheap scarecrow. The big man remained silent.

Harvey walked behind him. He felt Mad Bob's eyes follow him and saw them widen when Harvey bent to pick up the plastic bottle of fire starter.

"Are you two betting men?" asked Harvey.

Neither of the men replied.

"No?" said Harvey, answering his own question. "Okay, nor am I typically. But sometimes I enjoy a flutter when the stakes are high enough."

He turned the bottle upside down, stuck the nozzle inside Cannon Bill's shirt and squeezed a healthy amount of fuel onto the newspaper. Bill struggled, but Harvey held him still with one hand on the back of his collar.

"I bet," continued Harvey, "that one of you tells me where I can find your boss, or bosses, as the case may be."

Cannon Bill had begun to pant heavily. The smell of lighter fuel was heavy in the air, and he was sat just two feet from the fire.

"What about you, Bob?" said Harvey. "You like games, don't you?"

Bob glared back but remained silent.

"I'll ask the question once more," said Harvey as he began to spray a thin jet of fuel from the bottle onto the floor to form a circle around Cannon Bill. "Where can I find your boss?"

Lola began to get anxious and waved her arms. "Okay, this has gone far enough," she said. "Honestly, we'll deal with it. We can take care of ourselves."

"You asked for my help."

"Yeah, but we didn't know you were going to set light to someone," said Lola. "I can't be a part of that."

"You told me they shot your friend in the face?" Harvey held the bottle above Cannon Bill's head.

"They did," said Lola. "But, no, please don't do that."

"And you told me you can't go home because of the tag on your wrist."

Cannon Bill looked up at Harvey, his eyes wide with fear but masked with anger. Harvey had seen the look a thousand times and returned the stare. He squeezed the bottle. A stream of the flammable fluid ran onto Bill's face and soaked the newspaper stuffed inside his clothes.

"Fingers," said Harvey.

"What?"

"Can you count?" asked Harvey.

"Of course I can count."

"So count down from ten."

"No way. I'm not going to be a part of this."

"You *are* a part of this. Do you want me to let them go? Because I honestly don't mind. It won't be me they come after. You asked me to take care of them. Now I'm taking care of them."

Fingers stood open-mouthed.

"Count," said Harvey.

Fingers looked across at Lola, who turned her face away in horror, then nodded.

Harvey's eyes never left Fingers'. He held his gaze, unblinking even with the fire smoke, until Fingers gave in.

"Ten," he said softly.

"Where?" asked Harvey. He focused on his captive, but received no reply.

With a deft sweep of his wrist, he renewed the circle of flammable liquid around Cannon Bill.

Bill held his mouth closed, making it clear that he wouldn't talk.

"Nine," said Fingers.

Harvey smiled. "The thing you don't know about me is that I don't *want* to know where they are."

"Eight."

"I don't *need* you to tell me."

"Seven."

"I *want* to watch you burn."

"Stop this," said Lola.

"Six."

"I *love* to watch people burn," said Harvey. He doused the big man in fuel once more.

"Five."

"Fuck you," spat Cannon Bill.

"There it is. *There's* the anger," said Harvey.

"Four." Fingers was sounding nervous, but he continued the countdown.

"I won't tell you *anything*. You're going to have to burn me alive."

"Three."

"I cannot wait," said Harvey.

"No more," screamed Lola. "Just put it down. Everyone, just stop."

"Two."

"Last chance, Mr Cannon," said Harvey.

"No," pleaded Lola. "No more."

"One."

Mad Bob's phone began to vibrate inside Harvey's pocket.

CHAPTER ELEVEN

"Bob?" said Rupert. "Where are you?"

Mad Bob didn't reply.

"Bob, it's Rupert. Listen, do me a favour and steer clear of the little tart. I need her in one piece. So whatever you do, don't listen to my brother. Do not scare her off. Do you understand me?"

Silence.

"*Bob?* Can you hear me?"

Suddenly the tiny speaker inside the phone roared into life with the agonised screams of what sounded like a wild animal.

"Bob? What are you doing?"

Rupert held the phone away from his ear and gave his brother a confused look.

"What's wrong?" asked Charlie. "What's that bloody noise? I can hear it from here."

Rupert began to shout into the phone. "Bob? Answer me."

The shrieks grew louder and came in waves, as if whoever was screaming was writhing and rolling on the floor.

Then somebody spoke above the din, calm and controlled. "Which one are you?" asked the voice.

Rupert was appalled at the audacity of whoever the man was. His heart surged into overtime, and his face began to turn bright red.

He was too angry to even think about words.

"You need to stay away, and call your pet dogs off," said the voice.

The screaming began to die down, but panicked breathing and whimpering could still be heard. The noise had an echo, as if they were in a hard-walled room with no carpet or curtains. It was the old factory Mad Bob had mentioned. Rupert was sure of it.

"You're trying to trace where I am," said the voice. "Don't bother. I'll be gone."

"Who are you?" asked Rupert.

There was a pause as if the man was considering his response. "A man who doesn't like bullies."

"Are they dead?" asked Rupert. "My men?"

Charlie placed a crystal cut tumbler of scotch on his brother's desk. The lamplight formed ornate amber-coloured shadows that seemed to rock back and forth on the surface of the wood, before slowing to a stop.

"No," came the reply. "Not yet. Their lives depend on what you say next."

"What I say next, my friend, depends on the question, doesn't it?" replied Rupert.

"There's no question."

"So I'll say nothing."

"Then they die."

Rupert heard the inhale of a sharp breath when the words were spoken, distant, as if someone stood beside the man.

"You're with the girl."

There was no reply.

"Listen, pal," said Rupert. "I don't know who you are, and I don't know how you're involved, but you're muddying some very unsavoury waters. You have no idea who you are dealing with."

"If I wanted to know who you were, I'd have asked, wouldn't I?"

Rupert considered this comment.

The man continued. "And if I was worried about muddying waters, savoury or otherwise, I wouldn't be involved, would I?"

Rupert remained silent.

"And if was scared of who you might be, and what the consequences were, I wouldn't have burned your bloke's face off, would I?"

Rupert closed his eyes. "You burnt his face off?" he asked quietly. "Which one?"

"The one with the big mouth."

Rupert mouthed Mad Bob's name to Charlie, who was busy on his phone. He nodded in reply and continued to round the men up by messaging each of them.

"So what now?" asked Rupert.

"You let the girl go, I let your dogs go, you won't hear from me again, and the girl doesn't hear from you again."

"Oh no," said Rupert. "You see, we have a reputation to uphold. What would the world think if they found out we just let someone like you show up out of the blue, mess with our plans, and then disappear? Imagine what it would do to our credibility."

"So your boys die then."

The call disconnected.

Panicked, Rupert hit redial. His heart pounded. Rage soared through him.

The call was answered, but no greeting came.

Rupert swallowed his drink in one hit and placed the glass back on the table. "Do you think they're the only men we have working for us?"

"Probably not. But you trust them, more so than the rest."

"They're good men," said Rupert. "I've known them a long time."

"Are they worth a diamond?" the voice asked.

"No," replied Rupert. "But I'd gladly give the man that cuts your throat half of what it's worth."

There was no reply. Rupert heard the shuffling of boots on concrete. Mad Bob's whimpers grew louder in the phone and then a sickly gargle of another man choking on his own blood was clear as day in Rupert's ear. It was a sound he'd heard a dozen times before.

"My guess is that you've got every man you can spare on their way here right now," said the man.

Rupert stayed silent.

"You won't find *me*, so you won't bother looking."

"Is that right?" said Rupert. He raised the glass for Charlie to refill then signed with his finger across his neck that Mad Bob was dead.

"It ends now," the man continued. "Life goes on. I'll spare Mr Cannon here. He's having a rough night."

"No, son," said Rupert. "That is where you are wrong. You have, in fact, just entered a whole world of pain, and when I get my hands on you, you're going to find out what pain is." Rupert let his words sink in. "Do *you* understand *me*?"

"I understand you clear enough," replied the voice. There was a noise of movement on the phone, sudden and violent. The girl screamed and howled louder than before, and another man began shouting, but Rupert couldn't make out what he was saying.

The gargling sound faded to a stop.

Rupert didn't speak. He knew that Cannon Bill had just been killed. He pictured the scene. Lola LaRoux still screamed, and she had begun to cry hysterically with loud sobs and the heavy, anxious breathing of a child.

A silence fell between the two men until Rupert could finally bear it no more.

"You just started a war, mate."

CHAPTER TWELVE

The fishbowl was the nickname that one particular team of secret intelligence operatives gave to the small glass meeting space at one end of their operations room. Inside was a small table with four seats. The corners of the ceiling had foam cubes to prevent echo and the glass was half an inch thick and soundproof. Outside in the operations room, along the length of one wall were three banks of wall-mounted monitors, below which sat a row of tech researchers, including Reg's girlfriend, Jess.

Behind them in the centre of the room were logistics, comms, and team leads, all lost in their own worlds and oblivious to the very secret investigation with which Melody had been tasked.

Melody pulled the blinds down in the fishbowl, while Reg laid out the CAD files of the Natural History Museum.

"Impressive, isn't it?" said Melody, catching Reg admiring the detail that had gone into the drawings. "They were all transferred to digital a few years ago when the museum was extended," she began. "I can only guess that the thieves have the same drawings."

Reg smiled at her.

"Welcome back to crime fighting, Mr Tenant," said Melody. Then she turned her attention to the plans. "Right, well as far as I can tell the diamond is held in this room." She indicated to a small alcove of the museum's main gallery on the drawing. "We'll need to go there to identify the actual placement, but we can see on this MEP drawing that there's network cabling to this point here and this point here, both at high level." Melody indicated the spots on the technical drawing with an immaculate fingernail.

"CCTV probably shares the same cabling," said Reg.

"I think so too," said Melody. "But we need to be sure. I believe the museum also has a state-of-the-art firefighting system that runs off both network cabling and the original copper wiring."

"So that's the room. But what we need to find out are the entry points and the security weaknesses," said Reg. "They may have gotten into the old house to steal the first diamond, but this is the Natural History Museum. It's going to be virtually impossible to get in there and get out with one of the most expensive diamonds in the world."

"So we have the where. Now we need to work out the how and the who," said Melody. "The how is both the logistics and the technical aspect. Are you able to hack into the museum security? Could you give me a breakdown of what you can control and what you can't?"

"Yeah, I did that already," replied Reg. "I've still got a bit more to do, but as far as I can see, there's two or three layers to the security."

"Two layers?"

"Yeah, think of it as two networks," Reg explained. "The first layer is the public layer. It uses a network of fibre and category six cabling around the building. This is where the wireless access points will broadcast free internet access to the public, and where the screens around the museum will be fed the video feeds from media servers."

"Isn't that what the CCTV runs off too?" asked Melody. She had located the network of cabling that Reg was talking about.

"Nearly," he replied. "The next level is the CCTV and alarm systems for the displays. These will utilise the same back-bone infrastructure as the public-facing devices, but they'll be segregated at the switch level."

"Switch level?" asked Melody. "Less technical please."

"Okay, so imagine all the devices, wireless, alarms, CCTV, everything running to a single room on each floor, and they're all connected to one device; this is called a switch. In this instance, it's not just one switch. We're talking about thirty or forty switches."

"Thirty or forty?"

"Well, yeah. There's so many devices out on the museum floor that you'd need thirty or forty switches to connect them."

"Okay," said Melody. "I'm kind of getting that."

"Okay, so each switch or set of switches is controlled by a security interface. This segregates the devices into separate networks based on their function. So you could have all the CCTV cameras in one network, all the wireless access points in another-"

"Okay, I see where you're going," said Melody. "So all the devices essentially use the same cabling, but they are cordoned off at the switch."

"Exactly. That leads me to the second layer in the security design," said Reg. "The private network. We have the public network with all the WIFI and media stuff, then we need a secure network for the CCTV and alarm sensors, which are all fed to the security control room."

"Where is the security control room?" asked Melody.

"At basement level." Reg lifted the ground floor set of drawings and circled the security room on the basement level with a well-bitten fingernail.

"So that's where they control the alarms?" asked Melody.

"Yep," replied Reg, "the alarms, the sensors, the cameras, you name it, if it's security based it'll be controlled from in there."

"So you think our thieves will hit the control room?"

"I don't see that they have any other option. There's not many people that could get through the layers of security from the public network, so it'd be easier for them to take control of the control room, probably quicker too."

"Not many?" asked Melody. "So it *is* possible then?"

"Oh, it's possible. But there's only one man I know that could do that without triggering the alarms."

"One man?" asked Melody.

"Me," said Reg with a smile. "But I'm not going to be the one that robs the Natural History Museum."

CHAPTER THIRTEEN

"How are you feeling?" asked Fingers.

Lola raised her head a little and sighed.

"Like I just saw the love of my life shot in the face, and was then threatened with death or prison."

"What did the Bond Brothers say about Mad Bob and Cannon Bill exactly?"

Lola sensed he was trying to take her mind off the Dynamite incident.

"Do you want the long version or the short version?"

"Short first," said Fingers.

"I told them we don't know who the bloke was-"

"Which we don't."

"Right, he just came out of nowhere. I told them he must have been homeless or something," said Lola.

"Okay and they believed you?"

"I don't know, but it's true. We don't who he was."

"And what about the other diamond?"

"They still want it. They said that they'd decide what happens to us once they have it, and see how well the job goes."

"And what about the bloke?" asked Fingers. "Are they going after him?"

"They won't stop until they find him, Fingers."

"Do you think he'll come?"

"I told him where to find us, but I doubt it. I mean, would you?"

"How much did you offer him?" asked Fingers.

"We didn't talk about money. Somehow, I think he's not the type to be motivated by cash. I think he has other issues."

"You think? Lola, he set fire to Mad Bob's face. How else would you explain that?"

"Anyway," said Lola, "I doubt he'll come. I'm glad he was there, and that he stepped in, but-"

Her thoughts trailed off to Dynamite.

Fingers was silent for a while, choosing to take the dirty plates and cups to the tiny kitchenette at one end of the little houseboat. He returned to the small living area and hovered over Lola.

"Where did you get all this lot from?" he asked, as he ran his hands across the rolls of paper stood upended against the wall of the houseboat.

Lola glanced back from the window above her then saw Fingers was referring to the rolls of technical drawings. "I borrowed them," she said distractedly. She returned her attention to the huge sheet of paper spread across the small dining table. She held a magnifying glass over the paper and traced the tiny lines that represented the security network.

"Have you come up with a plan yet?" asked Fingers. "Time is running out you know."

"So why don't you help?" said Lola. "I'm here tracing networks and security, and you're sat there waiting for a diamond to fall out of the sky."

"Tracing networks?" said Fingers. "Don't be silly. I've done all that. It's easy, even easier than that soppy old bloke's house."

"Easier?" said Lola. "This is going to be bloody dangerous. I do not want you thinking it's easy and relaxing; I want you to be worried. In fact, I want you to think one hundred percent of the time about how bloody hard this is going to be."

"Alright, alright," said Fingers. "Get me close, connect a laptop to the internal network and I'm away. From there, I'll need about ten minutes."

"Ten minutes?"

"Yep, I told you, it's easier than you think. Just because there's a bloody great diamond inside, doesn't mean to say that it's any more secure than anywhere else," said Fingers. "In fact, it's not the digital security I'd be worried about. I'd have said the physical security is a bit trickier."

Lola nodded.

"I agree. There's five guards there at any one time, and another God knows how many close by."

"Apparently there are a few paintings on the walls that are worth an absolute mint," said Fingers.

"Not to mention the antique vases and statuettes," said Lola.

"Are we going to be taking anything else? You know make the trip worthwhile?" asked Fingers.

"No," said Lola. "Absolutely not. We get the diamond and we get out."

"Not even a nice little something to hang over the fireplace?"

Lola gave him a severe look. "I'm not doing this for money, Fingers," she said. "I'm doing this for Dynamite."

"And your freedom," Fingers reminded her.

Lola subconsciously rubbed the tag on her wrist. It weighed on her as if it were made of lead and hanging around her neck. "If we're caught doing this, Fingers-"

"I know, I know. We'll be fed to the wolves."

"We have a chance though, right?" she asked.

"Of pulling this off?" replied Fingers. "Yeah. Look, if you can get me access to the internal network, I'll need a few minutes to crack the security, and then I'll open the whole thing up. Once I've done that, I'll have access to the security console. The only question is how big the window is for you to get in and out."

"Don't worry. I have an idea about that."

"Sounds ominous."

"What's the minimum window you can give me?" asked Lola.

"Honestly?" said Fingers. "How's zero?"

"I won't know until I'm in."

Footsteps on the boardwalk above caught their attention. They saw the boots of their mystery saviour walking slowly along the length of the boat through the narrow portholes. The door opened with a slight creak, and two thuds of heavy boots resonated through the boat's wooden floor.

"I'm in," said the man. "Where and when?"

Lola felt a wash of relief run through her, but kept her eyes on her work. "I'd greet you, but you haven't told us your name yet," she said, without looking up.

Fingers edged away from the man and tucked himself into the corner of the sofa and against the wall behind him.

"Is this your boat?" asked the man.

"Does it matter?" Lola replied.

"Depends, doesn't it?" he said, as he stepped into the dining area. He seemed to loom over the room. His presence almost cast a shadow, though the grey sky outside cast little in the form of daylight.

Lola's eyes followed his until they felt like they would roll around in her head. She leaned back in her seat to get a better view of him and folded her arms.

"Depends on what?" she asked.

"Well, if you're planning to rob the Natural History Museum using a house boat that doesn't belong to you, the plan poses an element of risk that we don't need."

"It's mine," said Fingers. "It's where I live."

The man nodded, and eyed the kitchen mess.

"We?" Lola asked the man. "So you're now including yourself in this, are you?"

"You asked for my help," he said. "I came."

Lola remained silent. She studied his gestures and expressions, a skill Dynamite had taught her, to learn what really goes on inside someone's mind. The man had no tell signs.

"Harvey," he said suddenly.

"Harvey?" Lola repeated.

"Harvey Stone."

Lola repeated the name over and over in her mind. She was sure she hadn't heard it before, but it was strong name, a reliable name.

"It is Fingers' boat," said Lola. "We're safe here."

"Are you being watched?" asked Harvey.

"By who?"

"The brothers," said Harvey. "I'm pretty sure they'll have eyes on you, and will be waiting for me to arrive."

"So?" said Lola.

"So, I won't stay long," said Harvey. He turned to leave. "I just came to tell you I'm in. Tell me where and when." He paused. "You do still want my help?"

Lola's lips clamped the tip of her tongue in thought.

She nodded.

"Tomorrow afternoon. Five o'clock. Meet us at the junction of Denmark Hill and Daneville Road."

He nodded in reply, pushed the door open, and took a step outside.

"Harvey," said Lola, just as he ducked his head. He turned to face her. "Thanks."

He gave her a thoughtful look, nodded once, then left.

Fingers watched Harvey's boots walk back past the houseboat. He waited until Harvey was out of sight before speaking. "You really think he'll help us?"

"Gut feeling?" asked Lola. "Yes, I do."

"Why?" asked Fingers. "Why would someone get involved in something like this? And how can we trust him?"

"I don't know Fingers, but if we can deliver the diamond *and* him, I think we might just get out of this alive."

CHAPTER FOURTEEN

A narrow footpath ran alongside the canal so Harvey took it, preferring the peace and tranquillity of the waterway to the honking of horns and perpetual rumble of engines and traffic on the main roads. Two women pushed babies in prams. A cyclist rode by, and a jogger ran lightly past him. How normal people's lives were, thought Harvey. Most people had complications, of course. He knew that; he wasn't naive. But the complications of everyday people were usually along the lines of earning rent money, paying bills, fighting over custody of a child, or maybe, going to a workplace they hate every day and spending the smallest amount of time at home with loved ones before going to bed, only to do it all again the next day.

Harvey knew he was lucky not to be bogged down by such complications. But normality still appealed to him somehow. In the factory, he could have just stayed out of the girl's troubles. He could have just ignored the two men as they crept across the factory floor. He hadn't even needed to kill them. But it was who he was. Something had taken over him.

Killing was what he was good at.

Harvey took a seat on a bench while thoughts rolled around

his mind. The bench looked like the type of place that the local authorities had installed so that families could sit and feed the ducks. Instead, it had turned out to be a place where local kids could sit and get high without the prying eyes of parents.

The two women with prams walked past, deep in conversation. They took slow steps as if they had all the time in the world or too much to say and not enough distance to say it. They looked happy. Harvey watched them and couldn't help but think of Melody. They were supposed to have their wedding soon. Harvey knew that she'd wanted to have children as soon as they were married.

He pictured Melody in the place of one of the mums.

She would have been a good mother. Hopefully, she still will be one day, thought Harvey. But he doubted his own suitability to be a dad. A kid shouldn't have to grow up with a father who had spent most of his life as a hitman for a crime firm, and the rest of it on the good side of the law. But still killing. He was cold-blooded.

How could he possibly raise a child?

During the three months Harvey had been lying low, he'd had a lot of time to think, and to contemplate his future.

His decision to leave the crime world behind and live alone on his farm in France with a simple routine had been the outcome of many dark nights walking the rain or staring at the ceiling of his bedsit. But there had always been something gnawing at the thought. He knew what it was. It was a phrase he'd said to Melody once to describe how killing had made him feel.

"I enjoy it," he said aloud to himself. His voice sounded loud in contrast to his thoughts.

"*Excuse me?*" said one of the women as they strolled past.

The woman's voice shook Harvey from his daydream. His reaction was to offer a weak smile and wave the comment away as nothing. They walked on with furtive glances over their shoulders at the man sat talking to himself on the bench where kids get high.

"I enjoy it, and it's what I'm good at," Harvey said again. He repeated the words as if saying them aloud was somehow more convincing than losing them in the jumble of thoughts in his head.

"You've got talent," said a memory, somewhere distant in a dark corner. But this time it wasn't his own. "You're unique, Son. Don't waste it."

It was the voice of his foster father, words he'd spoken many times.

Harvey had been training with Julios in the gym at the back of their grand house in the Essex countryside. He had loved that gym. It had everything he needed to train with floor-to-ceiling glazing around the entire room. Even on the dullest of days, when the grey sky felt just a few inches out of reach, the gym had been full of light with no shadows.

Nowhere to hide.

John Cartwright made a habit of watching Julios train Harvey, while sat on the sun beds around the pool and holding a brandy between his fat fingers. When Harvey had developed into a strong sixteen-year-old, with two kills under his belt, John had watched and praised the boy's progress. When they'd finished training, all Harvey had wanted to do was to sit and eat with Julios and listen to a story of when his mentor was young. It was Harvey's favourite time of the day.

One time, they stepped from the gym, both boy and mentor glazed in sweat, and John had put his arm around his foster son and stolen the moment from Julios and Harvey. The mentor was made to stay behind and clean up. Instead of tales of Portuguese back streets and fishing on the Mediterranean,

Harvey had to sit with his foster father and listen to his dreams of what Harvey might be.

Harvey didn't need to hear the praise, he didn't need the push, and he didn't need any more direction. His path had been set in stone. He thought like a beast, with cunning and foresight, and he trained like a beast, with relentless vigour. Harvey had been building a pool of stamina to call upon when Julios pushed him to the edge. He knew he'd already become a beast.

"You're going to be a dangerous man when you get bigger, Harvey," John had said, as they'd sat in the kitchen eating.

In his mind, Harvey had recalled how he'd reached out from the darkness and slit his second victim's Achilles tendon before standing over the much older man.

"I can see it, you know?" continued John, as he shovelled carrots into his mouth. "I can see it in your eyes. And if you follow my advice, do what I say, you'll be feared throughout London. Maybe even further, who knows?"

Harvey chewed his vegetables. He avoided eye contact with his foster father, but let his mind continue to cast images in horrific flashes. First, there had been the boy from school, the sex pest who Harvey had hunted, found, and then slaughtered. Then came Jack, one of John's men. Julios had accompanied Harvey that time. He'd stood in the shadows and watched Harvey bring his own flavour of retribution to the sick man who'd raped Harvey's sister.

"You see," John explained, ignoring the fact that Harvey hadn't replied once. "Some people in this world are born to sit in an office. Some are born to help others, like nurses and doctors. But some, Harvey Stone, are born to even the odds. These people aren't bad people. But if the world didn't have them, and the rest of the men were left to their own devices, well, it wouldn't be safe to walk the streets. They bring balance to the world."

Harvey pictured himself walking the dark alleyways as he often did at the weekends, seeking lowlife to practice what Julios had taught him. He made himself a potential victim of a crime and waited to be attacked so he could unleash his skills.

"You're one of those people, Harvey," said John. "You're special. Some might even say unique."

Harvey imagined what the Bond Brothers might look like. He knew their type; he'd been around people like that all his life. Too much money, inflated egos, and somehow they'd earned respect. He knew they fed off fear, all bullies did. Harvey also knew that they wouldn't stop looking for him. They might find him today, tomorrow or a year from now, but one day the episode would catch up with him. Unless he stopped them.

Harvey felt John's eyes burning into him.

"Don't waste it," said Harvey aloud.

Further along the towpath at the exact location he'd been given, Harvey climbed down the few steps to a small wooden boardwalk. The canal cut through the neighbourhood. It acted as a dividing line between the old run-down factories on one side and the new-build apartment blocks on the other. The entrance to the dock was over a small footbridge spanning the gap adjacent to an old lock. Manicured lawns and trimmed bushes bordered the quiet private roads and parking bays that stood between the residential buildings.

He pushed open the door to one houseboat and ducked inside to find Lola and Fingers poring over building blueprints. The boat smelled of damp wood and greasy food, likely from the used pans and plates in the kitchenette.

Fingers averted his eyes when Harvey looked his way, and Lola kept her head down, engrossed in the plans.

"I'm in," said Harvey. "Where and when?"

CHAPTER FIFTEEN

"We seem to have a dilemma," said Charlie to his brother. They were sat in the back seat of their Bentley. Both wore dark blue suits with white shirts. The only differentiator was the colour of their accessories. Rupert wore a yellow pocket-handkerchief and tie, while Charlie had opted for a light blue.

"There's no dilemma, Charlie," said Rupert. "Merely plans to be made."

"We need to act, bro. We can't be seen sitting on our laurels while some nutter out there gets away with killing Mad Bob and Cannon Bill. It won't take long for word to get about."

Rupert stared out of the window as the streets rolled by. It always pleased him to see the dozens of small businesses that fell under his and his brother's protection. They had control over what was potentially a rough neighbourhood, and while petty crimes still existed as they would anywhere, most of the serious crime was dealt with swiftly and sharply.

"This is our manor, Charlie," said Rupert. "Look at it. Look how peaceful it is. When was the last time we ever had to step in and take care of anything here?"

"I don't know," replied Charlie. "Months ago, I guess. That bloke that tried to rob the betting shop, wasn't it?"

"Yeah, it was. I remember. But look how safe it is now. Look at that woman there on her own with her kids and all that shopping. A few years ago, she would have been ripe for a mugging. Nobody would have dared to walk down the high street with designer shopping bags. Even the teenagers on the corner of the street don't yell abuse at anyone who walks past. Can you remember what it was like, Charlie?" said Rupert. "Can you remember how diabolically crap this place was before we took over?"

"I remember, Rupert. But what are you saying?"

"I'm saying it's a bloody miracle, Charlie. That's what I'm saying." Rupert straightened his tie for the twentieth time and pulled his cuffs from his sleeves. "I'm saying that when all this is over, how long will it be before this place goes back to how it used to be? When women couldn't walk the streets without fear of being mugged or worse, and shopkeepers had to worry about being robbed every week just so some junkie could get his fix."

"Why are you dead set on leaving then?" asked Charlie.

"When I go, I want to leave a legacy. I want to leave this place better than how we found it. You know what I mean?"

Charlie gazed out of his own window with contempt as a scruffy old woman in slippers and a cheap coat with a cigarette hanging from her mouth stepped out of Better Odds betting shop.

"I couldn't care less what happens to these people, Rupert," he said. "What I care about, bruv, and something I think you've lost sight of is that somebody set light to Mad Bob's face and slit Cannon Bill's throat. And that certain somebody is out there somewhere thinking he can have one over on the Bond Brothers."

Rupert stared from his window in silence.

"What is it, Rupert?" asked Charlie. "Have you lost your bottle, or what?"

Rupert tore himself from the view of his world and turned to face his brother. "What do you reckon we should do then, Charlie, eh?" he said. "Why don't you tell me your master plan? You seem to be full of thought-provoking suggestions this morning."

"I don't care about thought-provoking suggestions, Rupert. Not when I know that scumbag is out there. I don't even need a plan. We get the boys to put the word out to find him and set light to him. See how he bloody likes it."

"Good plan, Charlie," said Rupert. "But it is those brash decisions that you are so fond of that wind up getting us into bother."

"Right and I suppose you have a master plan, do you? I suppose you plan to find him and give him a cuddle and a pocket full of cash and ask him politely to leave?"

"So what happens if we do find him?" asked Rupert. "We have the boys kick the crap out of him, maybe drag him round to Mad Bob's house so his family can have their say, and then to Cannon Bill's?"

Rupert paused and let the image run through his brother's mind.

"Then what?" continued Rupert. "You just scare the hell out of the girl, and she does a runner. Maybe worse, she calls the old bill."

"So what?" said Charlie. "Who cares about the girl?"

"So then here's what happens. The girl calls the old bill and the heat gets put on us, maybe they put the heat on someone a little more fragile than us, such as Smokey or Doctor Feelmore, and maybe the old bill finds the diamond."

"They can't prove it was us. We never stole it. None of our prints are on it," said Charlie.

"Even so, maybe the old bill turns the heat up anyway. Then maybe it starts getting harder to do business here. Maybe the police even start letting some other firm in, offering them more favourable deals. And then what? People begin to take the piss, Charlie, that's what."

Charlie shook his head and turned away as Rupert carried on.

"And even if none of that happens, even if the old bill don't come, and they don't find the diamond, and it's business as usual, by hitting the nutter that killed Mad Bob, you are going to scare the life out of the girl. And guess what?"

"What?" said Charlie, uninterested.

"She won't nick the other diamond for us, will she?"

"We'll sort her out too then. We'll hit them both together," offered Charlie.

"Don't be a moron, Charlie. If you hit her, she won't be nicking nothing. If you hit him, she won't be nicking nothing. If you hit either of them, we don't get the other diamond."

"The diamond?" said Charlie. He faced his brother. "The bloke just killed two of our best men, and all you can think about is the diamond."

"Charlie, the bloke just killed two of our men, yes. But, if we play this right, not only can we get our hands on the other diamond and leave this wonderful place behind, but we can also take care of the bloke, take care of the girl, and live happily ever fucking after. But mark my words Charlie; he will die a very slow and very painful death."

"You live in the clouds, Rupert. You know that?"

"I live in a world that I created, Charlie. A world where those who plan, live longest."

The car pulled to a stop in a bus lane in West London.

"And what is it we're doing here?" asked Charlie. "Another part of the master plan, is it?"

"I sometimes wonder how we actually have the same parents, let alone come from a single egg," said Rupert. "This building here is the Natural History Museum."

"What are we doing here?"

Rupert opened the car door and placed one polished brogue on the ground.

"We are learning, Charlie. That is what we're doing. Learning and planning."

CHAPTER SIXTEEN

"So that's it, is it?" asked Melody. "I thought it'd be bigger."

She sidestepped to allow a man and his two children to exit the small alcove where the diamond was displayed.

"Its reputation is bigger than this museum, Melody," said Reg. "Besides, it's not how big it is, it's what you do with it that counts."

"And what exactly would you do with that?"

The small alcove somehow shielded much of the ambient noise from the main gallery where the herds of schoolchildren and gaggles of tourists roamed free, so they were able to speak quietly.

"Retire," said Reg. "Tomorrow."

"You'd be even more bored than you are now," replied Melody. "I remember when you were signed off for two weeks after the Athens job, and you were on the phone every five minutes."

"I have an active mind, Melody. It needs stimulation. But I tell you what; I reckon I could stimulate my mind on a beach in the Maldives pretty well."

Melody gave a little laugh. "The Maldives, yeah?"

"Something like that. Somewhere warm with diet coke on tap and soft sand to rest my weary bones."

"Well before you get carried away with dreams of resting those weary bones of yours, Reg, how about you help me figure out this display cabinet?"

"That's easy," replied Reg.

He rested his hands on top of the glass. The lone Demonios Gemelos diamond sat encased in a small, round glass display unit resembling an upside down fish tank. It sat on an ornate pedestal as if it were a bust of Julios Caesar.

"See these?" said Reg, pointing at three small clips on the inside of the display. They looked as if they fixed the soft velvet cushion to the inside of the glass.

"Yeah, the clips?" said Melody.

"Not clips, Melody. These are sensors." He bent his knees to get a closer look. See in here, look, you can just see the ends of the two wires. Each of those three clips has a pair of wires that feed to the middle of the display beneath the cushion. They then run down the middle of the pedestal and into the floor void, where I imagine there are three separate alarm circuits."

"Three?" asked Melody. "Wouldn't they just run into one circuit?"

Reg stood from his crouch.

"No, that's the idea of having a round display," he explained. "There's no way on earth to lift one side of the display without triggering at least one other sensor."

"So if someone were to disable one sensor, surely they could disable the others?"

"They could, but the sensors won't be together and they aren't marked on the drawing as part of a display. Plus, displays move, right?"

"Right," said Melody. "So where are the sensors' alarm systems?"

"They'll be small black boxes," said Reg. "Each one of them will be connected to the private data circuit which is-"

"Security layer two," said Melody.

"And they'll also be connected to two power supplies running active passive."

"Active passive?" asked Melody.

"If the active power supply cuts out, the passive supply takes over. The sensor is down for less than two or three seconds."

"But doesn't that trigger the alarm? Surely the sensors are in contact with the security system?" asked Melody.

"Yes, but there's typically a tolerance to take into consideration the cut over between power supplies."

"So effectively, a thief would need to cut both power supplies on all three sensors to give themselves a two-second window to open the cabinet and steal the diamond?"

"Yes. But the diamond is also likely resting on a sensor of its own, which is held in place by its weight."

"Another sensor?" asked Melody.

"Any variation in weight within a given tolerance triggers a separate alarm." Reg smiled at the sheer genius of it. "And that's if they even manage to get into the building. This place has more security than Buckingham Palace."

Melody stepped around the display, her eyes never leaving the thousands of sparkles produced by the innocent-looking diamond.

"How would you do it?" she asked eventually.

"Me?" said Reg. "I wouldn't."

Melody gave him a glare. "If you had to?"

Reg began to play the scene out in his head. He looked up at the camera behind him then stared down at the floor and around the room at the other artefacts on display.

An ancient skull belonging to an African Masai warrior stared at him from behind the glass of a much taller display.

Various forms of early axes and stone tools had been carefully placed nearby. But the skull was the centrepiece. In another cabinet were carved items including tiny stones, hewn to a particular shape to suit a specific purpose. There were also small bird bones that had been used as awls centuries ago.

"Three tech guys," said Reg at last. "Three tech guys, two hard men to deal with physical security, and one man with balls of steel."

"So you're saying the thieves have six men?" asked Melody.

"No, but you asked how I would do it. Three tech guys, one for the power, one for the security, and one for the CCTV. I wouldn't even bother trying to disarm the alarms from here. They're all under the floor."

"You'd override the security and the power?"

"Easiest way. Once I get access to the remote security site, it's a doddle," said Reg. "The problem is that you still need to get inside the building and into the security control room, and you'd need to take care of the secondary security."

"Can't somebody guide the intruder using the CCTV?"

"For a while. But they'd need to shut the CCTV down. There's no way of knowing who else would be monitoring it."

Melody stood still, deep in thought.

"There used to be a diamond exhibition here at the museum, you know?" said Reg.

"There did?" said Melody. "I don't remember that."

"It was only open for a few months. Apparently the museum had some backlash from protesters about African tribes being forced out of their homes to make way for diamond mining."

"So they shut the exhibition down?"

"Well, shortly after that, the Metropolitan Police advised them to shut it due to increased risk of criminal activity," explained Reg.

"Increased risk-"

"Of criminal activity," finished Reg. "That's when they upgraded the security here. Makes me wonder if it's the same mob?"

"So what we're dealing with here is a group of highly-skilled criminals," said Melody. "That narrows the suspects down."

"Potentially, yes. However, most known villains that are even remotely capable of pulling this off are either dead or already in prison," said Reg. "I can't see it being done."

"Oh, it'll be done alright," said Melody. She was transfixed by the diamond. "If they have one of these already, there's no way they'll leave the other behind."

CHAPTER SEVENTEEN

"Here, Charlie," said Rupert. "Get Glasgow George on the phone, will you?"

"Glasgow?" replied Charlie. "It's eleven o'clock in the morning; he'll be in the pub by now having a liquid breakfast."

"Just do it, and trust me, will you?"

Charlie carried on walking, pulled his phone from his pocket, found Glasgow George's number and hit dial. "Do you want to talk to him, or should I?" asked Charlie. But Rupert wasn't beside him.

He'd stopped beside a display of some early hunting knives from around the globe, and feigned interest in a long curved blade of Damascus steel with a heavy wooden sheath.

Charlie stopped and took the few steps back to his brother with the phone in his outstretched hand.

"You talk to him," said Rupert. "I can never understand what he's bloody saying."

Charlie shook his head and put the phone to his ear. "What am I asking him?" he asked.

Rupert's eyes were focused on a man and woman stood either side of a large diamond in an ornate glass cabinet inside a small alcove off the main gallery. Above the arched entrance to the room was a model of an African tribesman and a sign with two words printed on it.

Demonios Gemelos.

Charlie followed Rupert's gaze and put the pieces together for himself. Rupert was transfixed.

"George?" said Charlie, breaking the tense silence that had built up in a few short seconds. "It's Charlie."

Rupert could hear the Scotsman's angry and slurred tone even from a few feet away.

"Yeah, yeah," said Charlie. "Listen, you remember the girl from the other night?"

Rupert watched as the man crouched beside the cabinet and seemed to gesture to beneath the floor.

"Yes, George, the diamond girl," said Charlie. "Do you want to say it any louder? There's a small tribe in a yet undiscovered part of the Amazon rainforest that didn't quite hear you."

Rupert listened to the one-sided conversation, but his eyes were fixed on the girl. She was looking up at the ceiling, perhaps checking the security cameras.

"What did she look like?" asked Charlie.

Rupert's eyes bore into the pair stood beside the diamond, picking up every little detail of their faces.

"Small," said Charlie, out loud for Rupert's benefit. "With long dark hair, and a face you'd want to take home to your mum."

It was her.

"And the bloke?" asked Charlie.

Rupert stared at the girl. She had a confidence in her manner and moved with the fluidity of a dancer.

"No, not the one you shot in the face. The other one."

Rupert turned his attention to the male.

"Short," said Charlie. "And skinny with glasses. Apparently, he looks like he needs a good meal."

"That's them," said Rupert.

Charlie disconnected the call and pocketed his phone.

"Shall we take a look?" asked Rupert with a raised eyebrow.

The two men strode into the small room, which somehow seemed to block all the ambient noise from the gallery outside. Charlie stood looking at the head of an ancient axe, while Rupert made his way to the cabinet that displayed smaller tools made from bone and rock.

He edged closer to hear the hushed discussion the pair were having, but could make out nothing. Charlie, who also feigned interest in the small rocks and bones, soon joined him.

"Three thousand years old," said Rupert.

"How do they know that?" asked Charlie. "They could have found that last week. The caretaker probably hit a bird with his car and put it in here as an exhibit."

Rupert didn't respond to his brother's retort.

He was watching the girl in the reflection of the display. It seemed to him that the dynamics of the conversation switched between the girl leading and the man taking control as if they were equals. Rupert moved closer still and studied the diamond in the glass cabinet from a few meters away.

"Shall we go and take a look around?" said the girl. "I haven't been here for years."

They slipped out of the small room and into the main gallery.

Rupert stepped out after them.

The ambient noise returned as if a switch had just been flicked, and a combination of smells hit him. The place smelled like a dusty attic with a hint of fried food.

He watched the pair walk away. They didn't look back. They didn't hold hands or link arms. All the time, the girl seemed to be glancing up at the huge expanse of ceiling forty meters above, as if checking for security cameras.

"Are you sure that's them?" asked Charlie, who had silently joined his brother at his side.

"Positive," said Rupert.

"I thought you wanted them left alone?"

"I do," replied Rupert. "But it's nice to know what they actually look like."

"You know," began Charlie, in a rare moment of reflection, "in the olden days, we'd of hacked their heads off and put them up on spikes so everyone would know not to mess with us."

Rupert gave a little smile. He enjoyed the fact that the only piece of interesting knowledge his brother could offer was on the subject of violence.

"Maybe when we've got the diamonds, that's what we'll do," offered Rupert.

Charlie's eyes narrowed into evil slits. "You think they were checking the place out? Maybe making a plan?" he asked.

"I'm certain of it," said Rupert. "In fact, that's what they're doing now. Watch them. She's checking the security, and he's on his phone."

"He's the tech guy, right?" said Charlie. "He hacked into the old geezer's place to get the first one, didn't he?"

"Yeah. I imagine what he's doing right now is finding a way into the security, so he can take it all down later."

The two brothers stared after the man and woman as they made their way along the first-floor mezzanine towards the two great staircases.

"I can't believe that one man and one woman could pull off a job this big," said Charlie. "Surely they'll need some help."

"If he's as good as Glasgow says he is," said Rupert, "and if she's as light-fingered as I hope, then I reckon they just might pull it off." He turned to face his brother. "But the truth is,

Charlie boy, I don't actually care if there's two of them or two bloody thousand of them. Because in less than twenty-four hours, that little tart over there will be handing me the other diamond, and we'll be richer than the bloody queen."

"I'm not really fussed about the money, Rupert," said Charlie. His voice had dropped to a growl, and he stared unblinkingly at the pair. "I'm going to nail her head to a stake."

CHAPTER EIGHTEEN

Harvey stood like a rock in a fast moving river as swathes of schoolchildren, families and tourists carved their way around him in waves of excitement and intrigue. Dozens of cameras hung from the necks of museum visitors, who posed for selfies and family pictures before the giant bones of a dinosaur.

It took Harvey a few seconds to scan his surroundings inside the huge gallery called the Earth Hall. According to the floor plan, pinned to a wall behind scratched Perspex, the diamond was displayed on the first mezzanine floor.

Harvey had no intention of visiting the diamond. Such a move would be like signing a confession, should the robbery go south. But nothing was stopping him from looking at the emergency exits and checking out the security.

With practiced and cautious movements, Harvey was able to identify the security cameras without being blatant about his research. Cameras seemed to cover every single area. The fire exits beside the washrooms were alarmed, the main entrance resembled a fortress, and security was patrolling every floor. The tiny room holding the diamond, an offshoot of the main gallery, had two cameras on the entrance and likely more inside the room, in addition to the sensors.

Harvey was keen to see Lola's plan. He saw two possible options for stealing the diamond. Although admittedly he was not a professional thief, he had experienced robberies and criminals for most of his adult life, and virtually all of his childhood.

Option one was to walk through the main door in the middle of the day, hole up someplace and wait for dark, have someone on the outside cut the alarms and divert the CCTV, then take the diamond and get out whatever way you could.

Option two was to storm the museum with ten to fifteen trustworthy men and take the diamond by force. The museum would automatically shut down if the alarms were triggered, making escape virtually impossible.

Both options were flawed. The museum sat in the middle of Kensington, London. The whole area was monitored day and night by Metropolitan Police CCTV control rooms based in Bishopsgate. A car wouldn't make it five hundred yards before the entire police force swooped in.

Harvey stepped back to the edge of the walkway and leaned against an ornate column. He felt eyes boring into the back of his head. A presence.

He turned slowly. His fingers found the moulded grip of his knife. The sheath had been sewn into the lining of his leather biker jacket. His trained reaction sent lightning-fast, multi-dimensional scenarios playing through his mind of escape routes and nearby weapons. He found himself standing face to face with a wax model of a Neanderthal man, who stood, ignorant of the reaction he had caused, behind the glass of a large, eight-foot-high display cabinet.

Amused by the idea of the waxwork model triggering his senses, Harvey smiled to himself.

He studied the man, with his furrowed brow, long wild hair

and strong jaw. The designers had placed him in a slightly crouched posture with one arm up, pointing at the far end of the hall as if some great danger lurked there, such as a predator making its way through the trees.

Harvey followed the Neanderthal's gaze. He saw no man-eating predator, no sharp teeth, no claws designed to tear the flesh off early man. Instead, he saw two identical tall men dressed in matching dark blue suits. They stood beneath the archway entrance of the small room where the diamond was being displayed.

The men stood motionless as a predator might. They stood at the edge of the alcove and were wildly out of place. It was the suits, the movements, and the way they interacted; they just didn't fit into their surroundings.

Harvey followed their gaze and scanned the herds.

A group of schoolchildren grazed on snacks from packed lunches, huddled in groups of three, while under the watchful eyes of two teachers, who seemed more interested in each other than the kids. Tourists formed small, closer herds and seemed to move as one along the edge of the mezzanine, flowing from display to display.

But two of the herd moved quicker than the rest, making their way towards the grand staircase at the far end of the gallery. They disappeared behind a thick column and reappeared briefly again on the other side.

The girl seemed alert, checking the ceiling space and voids. The man was occupied by his phone.

"Is that...?" Harvey whispered to himself.

He pushed off the wall. His senses pricked.

Harvey glanced back at the two men, who hadn't budged an inch but continued to sight their prey. He took a step back and fell in behind the column to watch from the shadows as Melody and Reg strolled down the huge staircase.

CHAPTER NINETEEN

"So how are we going to do this?" asked Reg, as he stepped from the last stone step of the museum's entrance to the pavement. "What's going on in that mind of yours? Now that we've seen the place, how are we going to catch them?"

Melody tried to refrain from beaming, but she allowed a hint of joy through pursed lips and showed a glimpse of her perfect white teeth.

"Why don't you tell me your plan first, and then I'll tell you mine?" said Melody.

"My plan? I think you'll find I asked first."

"Okay, but it seems to me that you're keener to hear my plan than I am yours." She skipped a small puddle of rainwater and put her hands in her pockets to make sure Reg knew she wouldn't give up her own ideas until he spoke first.

"Alright, alright," he said. "I gave it a lot of thought in there. To manage the security, the power and the data networks would need three men minimum. There's only one man I know who could handle all that himself, and he's standing right here talking to you. So we'll need to assume they'll have at least three tech guys."

"Copy," said Melody. "Physical security?"

"I said two inside before, but thinking about it, three minimum. One in the control room and two taking care of the guards. If they could have someone pose as a guard, even better. But I'm not sure how long they've been planning this, so let's assume not."

Melody nodded.

"Copy. What about the thief?"

"Like I said inside, Melody," replied Reg. "Balls of steel."

"How would they enter?"

"Loading bay. The only weakness I could find. The tech guys can deal with opening it, and from there the thieves could access the walkways that run behind the walls. They'd come right out beside the display."

"I saw that on the drawing. Do we know if security patrol the rear walkways?" asked Melody.

"We have to assume so. They'd have to force a few doors, but the tech guy could take care of the alarms, which would make the job much easier. If they took over the control room before the alarms were raised, they'd have free rein of the place."

"What if their hacker is good enough to control the security from outside?"

Reg's eyebrows raised as if the statement was a tall order.

"Then they'd have free rein all the way to the diamond, save for the guards."

"Okay," Melody replied. "Transport."

She knew the curve ball would trip Reg. He would have thought about the technicalities of the actual robbery, but not the logistics of the escape.

"This is West London, Melody. There's more armed police here than anywhere else in the UK."

"Yep," agreed Melody.

"Get away would be tough."

"Copy."

"In fact, it would be almost impossible."

"Mm-hmm."

"By car would be out of the question. You'd be shut down before you reached the main road."

"Agreed."

"By air might be good...But no, they'd have the police helicopters all over them in seconds."

"They'd be shot down," said Melody.

"Which only leaves the river," said Reg, as if in revelation.

"It does," said Melody.

"But where would they go from there? Surely the river police would be all over them?"

"It's harder to respond in a boat than by air or road," said Melody. "Besides, there are a hundred places they could dock and get out, only to disappear into the unknown."

"But how would they get there?" asked Reg. "To the river I mean. It's got to be nearly a kilometre from here."

"It's your plan, Reg," said Melody. "Why don't you tell me?"

"I don't know," replied Reg.

"Think about Harvey," she said.

"*Harvey?* What's he got to do with it?"

Melody didn't reply.

"Harvey?" said Reg again. Melody saw his brain engage. He always looked to the side through the gap in his glasses when he was in thought.

Then he fell in with what Melody was getting at.

"Motorbikes?"

"From here, straight onto Queen's Gate." Melody pointed at the junction a few hundred yards away. "From there, it's a straight road all the way to the river. On a motorbike, it's under a minute away."

"Motorbikes," Reg said again. "That means helmets too, so they'd avoid the cameras."

"If they have the right team, I'd say you just came up with a solid plan right there."

"It's all speculation, Melody," said Reg, deferring the praise. "We can't know how they'd do it exactly. All we can do is be ready for it when it happens."

"You think we can be ready for something like this?" asked Melody. "What are we going to do? Escalate the job and make sure the river police, the eyes in the sky and the response units are all lined up ready for the next two to three weeks? We don't know who they are, how they'll do it, or even when they'll try. All we can ascertain is that, given our experience and your knowledge of digital security systems, they stand a better chance of success if they go through the loading bay and into the service corridors. We also know that they're going to need three technical experts to control the cameras, the alarms and the power at the same time."

"There's one other problem," said Reg.

Melody gave him a sideways glance but didn't respond.

"I can't actually be involved. I mean, I can't escalate this. The job came from above and sits with you. If it needs to be escalated, and as you say, requires the river police, air support and armed response units to be primed, you're going to have to provide evidence for that kind of mobilisation. The chief isn't going to risk a massive waste of time and resources on a hunch based on experience."

"That's what I thought," said Melody.

"So what was *your* plan?" Reg asked. "Do you have something better than what I came up with?"

Melody gave a little laugh. "No. Actually, your plan works well, but we're missing something to make it work."

"Missing something?" said Reg. "You mean confirmed suspects and reliable data?"

"No," said Melody. "Much simpler than that."

She watched as Reg's eyes peered to the side of his glasses again.

"What?" he asked.

"A motorbike," replied Melody.

"A what?" said Reg. "Why?"

"Easy." Melody couldn't contain her smile any longer. "We're going to break into the museum."

CHAPTER TWENTY

The junction of Denmark Hill and Daneville Road was busy with early evening traffic heading out of London. A steady stream of commuters made their way from Denmark Hill Train Station or emerged from the continuous flow of buses that ferried people from the city or nearby underground stations.

Harvey thought it was a great place for a meet. Cars frequently stopped to pick up passengers or for passengers to duck into the nearby shops for a takeaway dinner. He leaned on the shutters of a closed shop while he waited for Lola and Fingers to arrive. The fact that he was about to rob the National History Museum didn't raise his pulse. He'd done worse things in his life. But the thought of getting his hands on the Bond Brothers tickled his excitement.

Lola hadn't mentioned what they would be driving. They'd find him. As much as he blended into the melee of commuters who stood waiting for buses or rides, he was easily identifiable to those that were looking. Those that weren't looking for him would pass as if he wasn't there. Just another face in the crowd.

A construction worker dressed in a t-shirt, dirty jeans and heavy boots with a green tool bag and spirit level stood adjacent to Harvey. He leaned on the shelter of the bus stop eating a bag of chips. Harvey smelled the salt and vinegar, and it reminded him of Fridays, the day when Harvey's foster father, John Cartwright, used to always demand fish and chips. He said it was a tradition. Friday was fish day.

An office worker dressed in a smart suit carrying a laptop bag stood behind the construction worker. He checked his watch then peered along the road for the bus before loosening his tie and opening a well-read newspaper.

Normal lives, thought Harvey. He wondered if they were going home to families or going home to be alone. He wondered if they might stop at a pub for a pint on the way, as many men used to do in John's pubs. Harvey had always wondered what it might be like to work in an office, to walk in at the same time every day and see the same faces. Maybe they'd ask how your evening was or what you have planned for the weekend. That all sounded very normal to Harvey.

But the chain that held them in that same room until five o'clock every night seemed restrictive. At the end of the day, what did they really achieve? What good did they do? It all seemed like a waste of time. Harvey had heard people talk of hitting sales targets, but it didn't make them wealthy enough to leave their jobs. They'd still have to go back and clamp the chains on the next day. They didn't help people, they didn't save lives, or-

Harvey's trail of thoughts jolted.

-make people suffer for their actions.

How many people had Harvey made suffer for their actions? How many grown men had he seen cry as he'd burned their limbs off in front of their own eyes? Sometimes, he did not even need to touch them before they shattered. Often, Harvey's words had broken men. He'd never threatened anybody; it wasn't his style. Threatening to hurt a big man would only antagonise him, but pulling out a confession, making them say the words out loud and admit the terrible things they'd done, that would destroy him. Verbalising the actions somehow made them all the more real. That was how to break most men.

Harvey wondered how he might break the two brothers. They would be different. Men of that stature usually were. They didn't typically perform the terrible actions. They only gave instructions and communicated their desired results. How the subordinate achieved the results was of no concern to men like the Bond Brothers.

John Cartwright had been the same. He would never have told Harvey to open a man up and pull his intestines out. He would merely state that he wanted a piece of information, and Harvey would extract it using the tools at hand, often using just his voice.

Mad Bob and Cannon Bill had been prime examples of subordinates. They were loyal and viscous, capable of almost anything, and guilty of worse than the construction worker with the fish and chips or the man with the newspaper could ever imagine.

Harvey had a clear picture in his mind. The two brothers had somehow learned of Lola and her team's plans to steal the diamond. Men of power, fuelled by greed, could easily intercept their escape. That was exactly what they had done, then stolen the diamond. It wouldn't have taken a genius to learn that the diamond was one of two, so they'd forced Lola to steal the second, which was a far riskier task than the first.

He could understand why Lola wanted Harvey to be part of the job. Her motive for that was clear; she wanted Harvey to protect her. She'd already seen what the brothers were capable of when they shot her friend.

But then what?

And where did Melody and Reg fit into the plans? Were

they investigating the first robbery, or preventing the second? Did they know about the second robbery, or was it a hunch? They were walking away from the Bond Brothers. Had they met? Were Melody and Reg somehow in cohorts with the villains?

Harvey wondered what Melody might do if she found Harvey at the robbery. Would she try to arrest him? How would he react? He could never hurt her.

Then two pieces of Harvey's puzzle seemed to come together to offer an alternative scenario. Harvey's chest tightened at the thought.

What would the Bond Brothers do if Melody cornered them?

A horn honked on the far side of the road. Harvey snapped back to reality. A four-door BMW was half pulling out of the side road. He could just make out Lola driving and Fingers sat beside her. Lola caught Harvey's attention with a discreet single wave of her hand.

Harvey shoved off the wall he was leaning on and made to cross the road, just as a large Ford van screeched to a halt in front of the BMW. The side door was thrown open, and two men in masks jumped out.

Harvey stepped into the road, watching the scene play out, deciding who to hit first. He focused on the driver of the van, who also wore a mask.

Another horn sounded, louder and closer. Harvey jumped back just in time as a large, red, double-decker bus came to a halt at the bus stop. Harvey was suddenly engulfed in people as they tried to board the bus. He shoved them away. All the time, his eyes watched the van on the other side of the road through the bus windows.

"Easy, mate," said the construction worker as Harvey began to jostle his way out of the crowd, knocking the man's dinner to the ground. Harvey ignored the comment, pushed free from the crowd, and stepped in front of the bus in time to see Lola being dragged into the van.

The side door slammed, the driver gunned the engine, and the van roared off in a squeal of tyre smoke. Harvey gave chase for a few seconds. He ran between the moving cars and dodged a man on a bicycle, but the effort was futile. The van turned into another side road and was gone.

Another loud car horn honked behind Harvey, followed by a stream of abuse. Harvey turned to find an impatient man behind the wheel of a Mercedes, gesturing that Harvey was mad by tapping his finger against his own temple and urging Harvey to get out of the road with wild waves of his other hand.

Harvey's head cocked to one side. He stared at the man through the windscreen and watched as the impatient anger turned slowly but surely to confusion, then fear. The driver slowly brought his hands down and stilled them. He locked the doors. As soon as Harvey stepped to one side, the man accelerated away with cautious looks in his rear-view mirror.

The world had just witnessed a kidnapping, but as soon as the van disappeared, life had returned to normal.

The BMW was also gone. But lying on the ground where the struggle had taken place was Lola's wrist tag.

CHAPTER TWENTY-ONE

"So, what's the plan?" asked Charlie. "Do you actually trust her to bring us the diamond?"

The two brothers sat in the back of their Bentley and passed over the River Thames on Battersea Bridge. Their driver kept the speed to a cool thirty-five miles per hour, giving his bosses a smooth ride in the style of which they'd grown accustomed.

"She has no choice but to bring us the diamond," replied Rupert. "She knows what will happen to her if she doesn't."

"And what about after?" said Charlie. "We can't just let them go free, not after what they did to Mad Bob and Cannon Bill."

"You're right," said Rupert. "And that's why we're not going to let them go free. She's going to meet us at Doctor Feelmore's funeral home, where she thinks she'll be handing over the second diamond and walking away with a fresh start."

"However?" said Charlie.

"However, we'll be waiting there to receive her, and when we get that second diamond in our own grubby mitts, she'll be taking a turn for the worse. We'll be handing all of them over to the good doctor along with all our troubles and sins."

"What about this other fella?" asked Charlie. "The new guy."

"Glasgow is putting the feelers out. If he's got any sense he'll stay low. But if he decides to come for us we'll be ready. Lola knows I want him. She'll stay well clear of him if she's got any sense."

"No, Ru," said Charlie. "It's too easy."

"Too easy?" said Rupert. "You want me to make it harder?"

"Alright, listen," began Charlie. "Picture this. You did a robbery with a mate and got away with a priceless diamond. I mean, I haven't seen it yet, but I'm guessing it's the last robbery you'll ever need to do, right?"

"Right," said Rupert.

"But on the way out, some better-equipped men with guns take the diamond off you, shoot your mate, and tell you to go get the second diamond. Oh and by the way, it's in the Natural History Museum."

"Right," said Rupert. "I'm following."

"So you do the second robbery, and somehow by some godforsaken miracle, you manage to get out alive and with the diamond. So for the second time in a week, you're holding the keys to a life of luxury. How did you put it? Sun, sand and semi-naked women?"

Rupert didn't respond.

"Do you honestly think for one second that you're going to waltz down to the local morgue to meet the blokes with the guns and hand it over to them?"

"If she's got any sense, yes. She'll want her freedom."

"She wants the diamond more, I bet," said Charlie. "She'd have to have a screw loose to give up a life of luxury. In one hand, she'd be Lady Lola LaRoux of some sun-kissed island in the Maldives, and in the other hand, she'd be Unlucky Lola of Peckham, the bird with a council flat who could of had it all, but didn't."

"You reckon she'd do a runner?" asked Rupert, doubting his own judgement.

"I reckon she might. But you know what, bruv?" said Charlie.

"Go on."

"I know for sure that if we're sitting on our arses waiting for someone to deliver us the second diamond, while they're skipping their way to Heathrow Airport, we'll be laughed out of London."

"Shit," said Rupert.

"You ain't the only one with brains, bro," said Charlie, sitting back in the fine leather seats with a smug look on his face.

"I hate it when you're right, Charlie," said Rupert.

"Don't beat yourself up," replied Charlie. "That's why there's two of us."

"You know London will be locked down if she does actually get out, right?" said Rupert.

"Yeah, we'll be quiet for a while," said Charlie. "We'll get the obligatory questioning from the plod, but they won't have nothing on us. No prints, full alibis and the rest. We'll let it blow over then we can talk about this sun, sand and semi-naked women thing."

"What's to talk about?" asked Rupert. "There'll be sun, there'll be sand, and guess what?"

"There'll be semi-naked women?"

"You'll be drowning in them, Charlie," said Rupert. "You mark my words."

The two brothers stared out of their own windows, both deep in thought. The day was drawing to a close, but the long summer sky still held hints of blue.

"I love London at this time of year," said Charlie.

"I like the blue sky," replied Rupert, but his mind was elsewhere.

Charlie gave a little snort of laughter. "The blue sky?" he said. "You carry on admiring the blue sky, bro. I'll carry on admiring the short skirts."

"Glasgow," said Rupert.

The driver caught Rupert's eye in the rear-view mirror.

"Yes, boss?" he replied.

"Do me a favour, drop me here," replied Rupert.

"What are you doing?" said Charlie. "We're miles away."

Glasgow George pulled the car to a stop in the bus lane, to the annoyance of a black taxi driver who was trying to pull out into the traffic.

"Is here alright, boss?" asked Glasgow.

"Perfect."

"Rupert, what the bloody hell are you doing?" asked Charlie, as Rupert pushed the door open and climbed out. Charlie leaned across and peered up at him.

"Charlie," said Rupert, feeling energised by his new plan. He enjoyed the flourish of confidence a new idea gave him. "Meet me at Doctor Feelmore's later and bring our passports."

"What about you?" asked Charlie.

Another taxi beeped its horn, and the driver gestured rudely at Rupert for stopping in a bus lane. Rupert gave the man a stare he wouldn't forget. The taxi pulled out around the Bentley.

"Me?" said Rupert, when the taxi had passed. "I'm going to make sure old Lola LaRoux delivers us from evil, bruv."

CHAPTER TWENTY-TWO

Car horns shook Harvey from his thoughts. He casually stepped to the side of the road, hearing but ignoring the angry comments that passing drivers made through open windows. The noise was just a background blur.

Were they too late? Had the Bond Brothers grown tired of waiting? Where did Fingers go? Was he scared? Was he in on it?

Harvey began to walk away from the junction. A girl had just been dragged from her car and thrown into a van; someone would have called the police, and Harvey couldn't afford to be questioned.

He ducked off the main road into an alley and pocketed the wrist tag. The alley led into a series of back streets that Harvey knew would eventually lead to the canal. He kept walking, using the time to think.

Walking away and leaving London as originally planned was an option. That was one thing Harvey loved about his life; he had options. First and foremost was the option to go home, put his feet up and forget about it all.

But forgetting was easier said than done.

He'd spent a lifetime dealing with bullies, hard men that preyed on the weak and gained from it either financially or in status. Harvey couldn't abide bullies.

Standing tall, a few hundred yards along the back street and adjacent to the main road, was a library. Harvey approached the building in thought. He pushed open the door and in a few sweeping glances had the place mapped out. The washrooms were in the far left corner with the fire exit beside them. In the centre of the large room, a middle-aged lady with glasses on her nose sat behind the curved reception desk. She didn't look up at Harvey. To Harvey's right was a bank of six desks with computer screens. Teenagers with books occupied two; the other four were empty.

Harvey took a seat at the furthest desk, facing the window and giving himself a view of the outside, with easy access to the fire exit. It was an old habit, but one that had proved useful on more than one occasion.

He clicked on the mouse button, which seemed to wake the computer up, and presented a box on the screen stating that the user agrees to the terms and conditions of the library's free internet usage policy. The terms and conditions looked long. There was no time for that. Even if he did break an internet law, it wouldn't be the worst thing he'd done.

Harvey opened the internet browser to begin his search. He started with the words, *Natural History Museum Diamond*, and hit enter.

The page filled with results. Some were about a diamond exhibition that closed just a few months ago due to police warnings about potential organised criminals robbing the place. Other results gave a brief description of single diamonds, and enticed the reader to click on the link to read more.

One of the results, close to the bottom of the web page,

briefly discussed a pair of diamonds, Demonios Gemelos, or Demon Twins.

Something twitched in Harvey's mind. There was a connection there that he couldn't quite grasp.

He clicked the link. Another web page opened up. At the top was an image of the two diamonds, the demon twins. Below the image was a single paragraph of small italic text.

Demonios Gemelos, or Demon Twins. A pair of 200-carat diamonds found in South Africa during the mid 1800s. The diamonds are believed to be cursed, bringing a quick death to any man that holds the two together. The diamonds have been separated since nineteen forty. One was donated to the National History Museum. The other was retained by the Abrams family, but was subsequently stolen in nineteen forty-eight.

Harvey ran an internet search for *Demonios Gemelos*.

Once again, the page filled with results for various websites all encouraging the internet user to click. But one result stood out from the rest. It stated that the missing Demonios twin might have been recently found. Harvey clicked on the link.

A new web page opened showing a stock image of diamond mining in Africa in the nineteenth century. The page went on to describe a pair of very precious diamonds discovered by a man called Roland Steinbach, who owned several diamond claims in Kimberly. Servants found Steinbach dead at his desk. Both of his hands had been removed, and the diamonds that he'd kept so proudly in a small safe were also missing.

Harvey went on to read that people believe the diamonds somehow ended up in the hands of a Dutchman who brawled with an Englishman and lost. The Englishman then took the diamonds as a gift for Queen Victoria, but he was drowned at sea. The captain of the ship stole the diamond and escaped with a few of the crew on a lifeboat.

However, the crew soon learned of the diamond and killed the captain before they washed up in Portugal. The three men found the British Army and requested safe passage to England. But before they left France, one of the men tried to steal the diamonds. He was caught and killed by the remaining two men. The two men agreed to carry one diamond each. They went their separate ways at the busy port of Calais, and never saw each other again.

One of the men, Jack Penn, sold his diamond to Hans Sloane, who eventually created the Natural History Museum and donated his huge collection of natural artefacts. The remaining diamond remained in the Abrams family up until nineteen forty-eight when it was stolen. Despite the Abrams' large offers of reward, it was never returned.

More recently, the diamond was spotted by a collector who wished to remain anonymous and is due to be sold at a private auction in the UK.

Harvey checked the top of the article. It was dated three days previous.

He opened a new web page and searched for *Stolen Diamond*. A fresh page of results appeared, and at the very top of the page, the headline read, *Missing Cursed Diamond Stolen*.

Movement outside caught Harvey's attention. Two armed policemen ran past the window of the library towards the door. Harvey closed the internet browser, ran the sleeve of his jacket over the mouse and keyboard, more out of habit than necessity, and then casually made his way toward the washrooms. He took a quick look around him then bolted for the fire exit.

The alarms sang out immediately.

The alleyway behind the library was clear, but neither left nor right was a great option. Harvey took a few steps forward then leapt up and grabbed onto the wall in front of him. He pulled himself over and dropped down to the garden on the other side. Dogs barked nearby, and he heard the heavy engine of the police arriving behind the wall. Car doors opened and radios sang as the police closed in.

Harvey tore up the garden. He ducked down the side of the house, burst through a garden gate, and found himself in a back-street. He glanced left and right, then bolted into an alleyway in front.

The thump of an approaching helicopter stopped him dead in his tracks. He dove for cover beneath a large bin and waited for it to pass, knowing that the police would be using infrared to find his heat signals.

Sirens sounded in all directions. Harvey knew they would close the area down, and he had to get out fast.

The whomp of the helicopter's rotor blades was suddenly deafening in the air above. His subconscious readied himself to fight. The familiar iron taste ran around his gums, and the tingle of adrenaline surged through his veins.

The helicopter hovered for a while. At the far end of the alleyway, a police car stopped. It as if the driver was daring him to move.

Harvey lay dead still, his senses alive, interpreting, planning and preparing.

But as fast as it had arrived, the helicopter banked and continued its search elsewhere. The police car slipped away, leaving an empty run of alleyways in front of Harvey, all the way to the canal.

Seeing his chance, Harvey slid from beneath the bin, checked around him then sprinted through the network of alley-ways. Slowly, the noises of the sirens and helicopters began to fade away, and eventually he burst onto the quiet canal-side footpath.

But Harvey didn't stop running. He ran with everything he had until less than a kilometre later he reached the factory where he'd first met Lola and Fingers, Mad Bob and Cannon Bill.

After finding the gap in the fence, Harvey kicked the door open and stepped through onto the factory floor. It was empty, as he knew it would be, save for the pigeons that scattered on his arrival. He wondered if Mad Bob and Cannon Bill had been found and their bodies removed. But he didn't stop to check.

Instead, he walked up to the pile of boxes and old pieces of machinery that were stacked to one side of the vast room. He pulled back the dusty tarp and breathed a small sigh of relief.

In the midst of the boxes of papers, greasy machinery and random factory objects, exactly where he'd left it three months before, was his beloved motorcycle.

CHAPTER TWENTY-THREE

"I can't believe you talked me into this, Melody." Reg's voice came across loudly over Melody's ear-piece. "This has got to be one of the stupidest ideas you've ever had."

Melody was crouched in the shadow of a tree one hundred yards from the huge rolling shutter doors that were the loading bay entrance to the Natural History Museum.

"You said it yourself, Reg," she began. "We're missing credible evidence and confirmed suspects. What better way to get both of those than to catch the thieves red-handed?"

"What makes you think they'll do it tonight?"

"They have one diamond already. Greed will have set in by now. The longer they leave the second hit, the harder it will be. All eyes will be on the museum's diamond and security will tighten. Anyway, we don't have facts, but we do have years of experience on our side."

"Melody, if you're caught, you'll be locked up," said Reg. "And I won't be able to get you out of it. You'll have years of experience in something altogether different."

"So let's not get caught, Reggie, eh?"

Melody heard Reg's sigh loud and clear across the comms.

"Let's just stay focused, Reg," said Melody. "Run through the plan once more."

"Okay," said Reg. Melody had worked with Reg long enough to recognise when his reluctance was tinged with a hint of excitement at the challenge. "I'm connected to the public network and I've accessed the remote security facility. From here, I can see all wireless access points and media channels. In a few minutes, I'll be onto the secure layer, which is the CCTV and alarms. Once that's done, I'll pop the single rear door to the side of the loading bay. That'll be your cue to go in."

"Copy," said Melody. "Any other locks?"

"No. The internal doors are all secure key card access that run off electromagnetic locks. I can isolate the power circuit that runs those doors and release them for you so you should have a clear run."

"Easy," said Melody. "What are you worried about?"

"What am I worried about?" said Reg. "Ah, let me see. Well, first off, there's not seeing Jess for the next ten years. Then there's showering with an entire wing of men much bigger than me who haven't seen a woman for God knows how long. Then, of course, there's the little thing of being locked in a tiny cell with one of them every night and becoming their sex slave."

"Anything else?" asked Melody, as she pulled her hood up over her head.

"I hear the food isn't great either," replied Reg.

"Are you finished?" said Melody.

"Finished listing the things that I'm dreading or finished opening the doors?"

"The doors," said Melody. "Your insecurities merely amuse me."

Melody could hear Reg's fingers tapping away at his keyboard. She had every confidence in his abilities.

"I'm glad I get to amuse you one last time," said Reg. "The

rear door is open, and the cargo area is free of guards for one full minute. You are good to go."

Melody darted the twenty yards to the building and edged along the wall to the small door. It sat inset into the brickwork to one side of the giant rolling shutters. She glanced up at the keypad; no LEDs were blinking. A small set of eight concrete stairs led up to the door, which opened easily and silently. Within a few seconds, she was inside, standing on a raised concrete walkway the exact height as the rear of the four trucks that were parked up below. Presumably, so the workers could easily push trolleys of fragile goods out of the truck cargo areas and wheel them inside the museum.

A goods lift stood open, full of dark shadows with a set of double doors to one side. A narrow pane of reinforced glass set into both doors showed Melody the empty corridor beyond.

"I'm inside. Is the corridor free?" she asked.

"For the next thirty seconds, you need to be in that corridor. Then move into the first turning on the right in under forty-five seconds," said Reg. "I've been watching the guards' movements. They seem to have a pattern. But from here on in I need to kill the CCTV until you're in position. Otherwise, you're going to have a dozen guards rush you from all angles."

"That's fine, Reg," replied Melody. "Once I'm in the service corridors, I should be okay. I'll hear them coming."

She pushed through the double doors and let them close behind her, just in time to hear another door open in the loading bay. A few cautious moments passed as she listened for any signs of movement. Then, once she was happy the coast was clear, she sprinted to the first junction in the corridor.

There was a smell of disinfectant. The long walls that trailed off in various directions were painted cream up top and green on the lower half. The concrete floor had been painted dark grey. Melody thought that the place was immaculate like a hospital but with a distinctly industrial feel.

The smaller corridor led to another set of double doors, beyond which was a staircase.

"Up the stairs?" asked Melody.

"You got it," said Reg. "Up to the first floor. The corridor up there leads left and right. You'll need to head right."

"Copy," said Melody, and pushed the doors open. Immediately, she heard footsteps coming down the stairs. She darted into the dark space beneath the stairwell and edged into the shadows.

A deep voice echoed from the stairwell walls, and the footsteps stopped.

"Yeah, I'm here. What's up?"

His radio crackled into life.

"Just had a call from control two, Stevey. They're saying the cameras are down. Be advised, mate."

"Again?" said the man apparently called Stevey. "They went down last week too."

"Just be on your toes, mate. That's all."

"Yep, will do."

The footsteps continued. Stevey's loud breathing disappeared when the double doors closed behind him. Melody made her move up the stairs.

"Sounds like they're onto the cameras being down, Reg."

"Get yourself in position and I'll turn them back on. They'll think it was just a glitch."

"I'm in the first-floor corridor. I turned right."

"Great. You should see that the corridor turns to the left about a hundred yards in front of you. The room with the diamond is the last door on the left-hand side before the bend. Get to the door but don't open it," said Reg. "I need to kill the alarm system first."

"Okay, sit tight." Melody ran the hundred yards as quietly as she could. "I'm outside the door," she whispered.

"I'm working on it," replied Reg. "Give me twenty seconds."

Voices approached from around the bend in the corridor. It was two guards discussing how antiquated the security was in the museum. Their voices grew louder.

"You need to hurry," whispered Melody.

"I'm trying Melody," replied Reg. "But I just found a bypass. The alarm sensors are well-protected."

"I have about ten seconds until I'm discovered and I have nowhere to hide," said Melody.

The two men's voices were so close now that Melody could hear their breathing. Their footsteps were slow and casual, not the footsteps of two guards who were on the lookout for trouble.

"Reg," said Melody, "come on."

"Okay, how about this?" said Reg. The lights in the corridor flicked off, leaving the long chamber in pitch darkness.

"What the bloody hell now?" said the first guard as he rounded the corner. "I can't see a bloody thing."

Melody pinned herself to the wall, making herself as thin as she could to let the two guards pass.

"Here, hold on," said the second guard, who sounded a lot younger than the first. A flashlight flicked on, illuminating the corridor in front of them as they moved past.

Melody stood motionless as the beam of light danced across the floor in front of the two men. It wasn't until they disappeared into the stairwell that Melody dared to breathe out.

"Nick of time, Reg," she said, as her heart began to calm down.

"Nothing to it," replied Reg. "You want some light in there?"

"It'd be nice," said Melody, just as the corridor lights burst on again. The hum of electricity she hadn't heard before became very apparent in the otherwise silent space.

"Try the door," said Reg.

"Are we good to go?"

"Only one way to find out."

Melody pushed the lever on the door handle and stepped into the live side of London's Natural History Museum.

CHAPTER TWENTY-FOUR

Standing in the shadows, silent and still, Harvey watched his ex-fiancé edge along the outside museum wall. Had he not known it was Melody beforehand, he'd have recognised her now from the grace and style with which she moved.

From where he stood, he couldn't hear her talk, but from her actions, she was waiting for something. Somebody would be accessing the museum security for her, clearing a path and guiding her through. There was only one man she knew who could do that.

Reg, thought Harvey.

Melody took the concrete stairs in a few silent steps and opened the small door to the left of the loading bay entrance.

Harvey gave his surroundings a final check then followed. He caught the door before it closed, and watched Melody through the tiny reinforced glass. She disappeared into a corridor.

Keeping his noise to a minimum, Harvey followed on her heels. He was in the corridor in seconds and waited at an intersection. He heard Melody talking on her comms to Reg. Her short, sharp comments over the stealth comms units were familiar to Harvey. It felt good to be so close to her. If it wasn't for the strong scent of disinfectant, he thought he'd be able to smell her familiar fragrance.

Her whisper faded away as she crept through the double doors into the next corridor. But a man's voice, loud and clear, echoed off the flat, hard walls. A few seconds passed as he stopped to talk on his two-way radio, and a loud crackle of a distorted voice announced that the guard had opened the doors and was heading Harvey's way.

The guard's footsteps stopped. Harvey chanced a glance around the corner and saw a heavyset man peering back through the doors.

He was pulling a telescopic cosh from his utility belt.

Harvey saw Melody dart from behind the stairs, and the guard began to re-enter the stairwell after her.

In three long, silent steps, Harvey had a hand over the guard's mouth and his arm bent behind his back. A sharp knee to the man's leg sent him to the floor.

The door closed silently behind Harvey, leaving the two men staring at each other.

"You have a family?" whispered Harvey, as he unclipped the man's radio, turned the volume down and pocketed it.

The guard nodded.

"Are you going to be quiet?" asked Harvey. He took the cosh, closed it and tucked it into his own belt.

The guard nodded once more.

In less than a minute, Harvey had the man's wrists zip-tied behind his back and his ankles bound with the laces of the man's boots. A sock was stuffed into his mouth and secured with a long length of duct tape wrapped around his head.

Harvey dragged him to the dark storage space beneath the stair well.

"If you be good, I'll tell someone you're here when I'm done," said Harvey. "If you make a noise, I won't be so nice."

He slipped away and bounded up the stairs after Melody, just as the lights flicked off, leaving the stairwell dimly lit by the hazy green glow of the emergency exit signs.

The first-floor corridor was pitch dark. Harvey stood in the doorway holding the door open and listened. Two men were talking to his right. Then a flashlight switched on and began to wave a fat beam of light around the corridor. Harvey closed the door and stepped back into the stairwell.

He stood to one side and waited.

The bouncing torch light announced the arrival of the two men and the double doors shoved open revealing one man in his twenties of medium build and an older, more portly man who Harvey placed in his fifties.

Harvey waited for the doors to close then struck the younger of the men hard to the side of his head with the cosh. He went down without a noise, and the torch fell to the floor with a crash.

The older of the men began to voice panicked questions. The white of his eyes shone bright green in the emergency lights.

"Who's that?" he said, clearly unready for an attack. "Jimmy?"

But before he could say anything else, Harvey had whipped the cosh back and slammed it into the man's temple.

Tying the men together using the last of his zip ties took a few minutes. He took their radios, removed the batteries, and dropped their mobile phones over the edge of the stairwell to smash on the concrete floor below.

Two more lengths of duct tape secured their mouths. The two men were still out cold by the time Harvey had finished. He tied them back to back with their wrists joined and a strip of tape wound around their foreheads.

Harvey admired his work for a second, and then pushed through the doors and stepped out into the corridor. The lights in the long empty space had been turned back on.

The corridor to the left was long and empty. To the right a few doors led off, and the corridor bent to the left. Presumably, the walkway ran around the perimeter of the mezzanine feeding the little alcoves Harvey had seen. He turned right and pictured the place where he'd stood earlier that day on the first floor of the gallery. If his judgement was right, the diamond display would be the last door on the left-hand side of the corridor.

With an ear to the door, Harvey listened. He knew he wouldn't hear anything; the doors were thick, and Melody would not be making a noise.

He pushed the door open slowly.

CHAPTER TWENTY-FIVE

Melody gazed at the perfect sparkles that reflected from the diamond's surface even in the low light.

"Pretty, isn't it?" said a voice behind Melody.

It wasn't just any voice. From the first syllable he spoke, she knew it was Harvey. Her mind recognised his tones and powered into overdrive. Her heart skipped and her chest tightened, then her knees felt weak as if they might give under the weight of his presence.

She froze and felt her gun being lifted from her belt.

"What are-"

"No questions," said Harvey. "You wouldn't like the answers."

"Then you're here to steal the diamond?"

Harvey didn't reply.

"I can't let you take it," said Melody. "You'll be shot dead before you step foot outside."

"I doubt that Melody," said Harvey. "Besides, *I* won't be carrying the diamond."

"You expect *me* to walk out of here with it?"

"That's an option."

"*No*, Harvey. It is not an option," hissed Melody. She turned to face him before he could stop her.

Their eyes met.

He looked gaunt and unshaven.

A silence grew between them that felt harder to break as each silent second ticked by.

"How have you been?" he asked. His voice had softened.

Melody swallowed what felt like the diamond itself.

"Don't do this," she whispered. "It's not you."

"It's a means to an end."

"An end?"

Harvey remained impassive for a few seconds then spoke quietly.

"Not my end."

Melody stared at the shine of his eyes in the soft light. The room was unlit, but enough light spilt from the main gallery for them to see each other and to bring the diamond's glittering surfaces to life beneath the glass.

"I can't let you take it," said Melody.

"It's not me that's taking it," replied Harvey.

"I miss you, Harvey. Don't do this."

"Take the diamond, Melody."

"You can't make me."

"What if I told you that I know who has the other one? The second diamond."

"It's not you then?" asked Melody, fishing for clues as to his motive.

"I'm not a diamond type of guy, Melody," replied Harvey. "You know that."

"So why then?" she said. "Why do this?"

"What if I told you a girl will die if I don't?"

"Who?" said Melody. "Tell me. We can help."

"You can help by lifting that lid and taking the diamond."

"I could scream. There'll be twenty guards here in a matter of seconds, and the police will be right behind them."

Harvey didn't reply.

"It might take some explaining, but I'd likely be okay. I can't say the same for you though."

"Am I still wanted?" asked Harvey. "Are the police looking for me?"

Melody shook her head and felt her eyes water.

"No, Harvey, no. You were *never* wanted. You're a free man. But do this, and there's no more I can do to help."

Harvey reached for his belt and pulled a telescopic cosh. He swung a short stabbing swing by his side and it extended with a series of sharp clicks.

"Move aside, Melody."

"Please, don't do this, Harvey. I can't watch you go this way."

"So move aside and get out. Run."

Melody stood her ground.

Harvey reached back with the cosh. Their eyes locked. He tensed and swung the cosh down.

"Okay, okay."

Harvey stopped mid-swing.

"I'll get the diamond," said Melody. "But you need to tell me exactly what's going on."

"I told you," said Harvey. "A girl will die. Help me save the girl, and you can have them both. You'll be a hero."

Melody let her head fall forward. She gave a sigh then looked up at Harvey. His eyes hadn't changed. His cheekbones were a little more pronounced, his hair unkempt and his beard was rough and scraggly.

Footsteps sounded not far away. It was the slow, bored pace

of a security guard following the same route he took a hundred times a night.

Harvey stepped away from the display case and dragged Melody with him. The pair stood chest to chest in the shadows to one side of the arch. Melody could smell his scent, familiar, warm. She closed her eyes and breathed him in, then rested her head on his chest.

Two boots stopped at the archway, as if they were afraid to step further.

Melody could feel Harvey's heart against her cheek. She felt his muscles tense as he made himself ready to pounce.

The guard stood a few seconds, then spoke to his radio. "All clear on mezzanine one. No sign of Stevey or the other two."

A short silence was broken by the scratch and crackle of the radio.

"Ah, no problem, Del," the controller replied. "They're probably skiving as usual."

The heavy boots turned away and returned to their slow, bored plod. The pair listened to the guard move off, and then both breathed out slowly.

Melody placed her hands on Harvey's chest. "Just like old times." She smiled.

Harvey matched her gaze. He bent forward, bringing his lips close to hers. Melody closed her eyes and waited for the soft familiar touch of his mouth. She felt his warm breath, and the way he rubbed her forehead with his own. Their noses touched just briefly.

"Get the diamond, Melody," whispered Harvey. "Then we'll talk."

He pulled away, leaving her hanging with pursed lips.

Melody watched as Harvey approached the arched entrance, being mindful not to step too close to the boundary that the guard had clearly avoided. He gave her a wave as if to tell her the coast was clear.

Melody took a deep breath and let it out slowly, then hit the little button on her ear-piece to talk to Reg.

"Reg, I need a little help here," she said.

CHAPTER TWENTY-SIX

A small tinny speaker crackled into life in the rear of the van.

"Reg, I need a little help here," said a female voice. "Are you there? Talk to me."

Rupert stepped up into the cargo area and glared down at the thin man sat in front of a small bench whose face was lit by a pair of computer screens. He slid the sliding door closed behind him.

"This is not the time to go quiet on me," said the girl, her voice a little more urgent than before.

The man sat motionless, his eyes wide.

"Can I answer her?" he asked.

Rupert nodded and placed a finger over his lips. His other hand held the gun to the man's head.

"I'm here." Then the man released the push to talk button, never removing his eyes from Rupert's.

"Where is she?" asked Rupert.

"The diamond display," replied the man. His voice quavered just a little.

Rupert lowered the gun, leaned on the back of the van's front seats, and nodded at him to continue.

"Reg, I need a little help," said the girl.

"Can I answer her?" asked the man again.

Rupert nodded again. "Do whatever it takes, but *do not* do anything stupid."

The man at the computer cleared his throat. He hit the push to talk and spoke quietly into the microphone.

"What do you need?"

A long silence followed then the girl replied with an equal tremor in her voice.

"The alarm is on the display," she said. "You still think you can get me a window?"

Rupert's eyes were locked onto the man's.

"How long do you need?"

"Max ten seconds," said the girl.

"It'll take some doing, but I think so." The man shifted in his seat and began to tap on his keyboard. "Have you run into difficulties?" he said into the mic.

"You could say that," replied the girl. Her voice was tinny over the comms and blocked in part by the museum's thick walls.

He released the button and turned to face Rupert.

"I need to get busy," said the man. "It might take a few minutes."

"Go ahead," said Rupert. "I'll be watching. No funny business."

From where he stood, Rupert could see the screens. The man was typing into a black interface. White text flowed in streams of what looked like code. Although Rupert couldn't understand the commands, it was clear that the words were computer talk.

Another interface opened, which looked like an internet browser. A username was entered followed by two failed password entries in quick succession. A message displayed informing them that a third failed attempt would lock the user out.

"You know the password?" asked Rupert.

The man tilted his head back as if in thought, then gave a huff, a spit of keystrokes, and slammed the enter button down.

The screen went blank then re-opened into a graphical representation of what looked like symbols for electronic switches.

"What's that?" asked Rupert.

"These are the sensors placed around the various displays in the museum."

"All of them?" asked Rupert, slightly impressed.

"As far as I can tell."

"So which ones do we need?" asked Rupert.

A few clicks of the mouse and the screen showed a 3D model view of the museum as if it had transparent walls.

The man zoomed in, rotated the view, and then zoomed in some more, until a vague resemblance of the alcove with the diamond display was on the screen.

There were nine sensors in the room. Two were beneath the floor of the entrance under the archway. The man waved the cursor over them.

"Pressure sensors," he said, as if to confirm the obvious to Rupert.

He then moved the cursor to the sensors on the walls.

"Artwork, cabinet, and then the other cabinet and one more piece of artwork."

Rupert remembered the pictures on the walls beside the cabinet containing the stone tools. They'd been photos of ancient cave paintings found somewhere in Africa.

"That leaves three," said the man. He brought the cursor to the three sensors that seemed to float in the air to form a triangle.

"How long?" said the girl. "It's not a good time for me here."

The man reached forward and hit the push to talk button.

"I'm close," he said. "One minute, and for the record, I'm not exactly having a ball."

He released the button. Then he stared at the screen.

"So you can disable the sensors?" asked Rupert.

"I can disable them okay, but they have a backup sensor which will need to be disabled first."

"Where's the backup?" asked Rupert.

"It's hidden beneath the cushion."

"How do you know?"

Rupert's comment seemed to aggravate the man.

"Because I looked, and I'm not stupid."

"You've done this before?" asked Rupert with a smile. "But how do I know you're not trying to bluff me?"

"Listen, I don't know who you are, but my friend is in there, and I'm going to get her out without this place lighting up like a Christmas tree and half of London's police carting us all away."

The two men stared at each other in the dim light.

"Now," the man continued, "are you going to carry on asking questions, or can I just do this?"

"I'm running out of time here," said the girl over the comms.

"Don't pull any tricks," said Rupert.

"Can you at least lower the gun?" said the man. "This is tense enough without having that thing in my face."

"I'll lower the gun when the diamond is in my hand," replied Rupert.

The man exhaled audibly then returned his attention to the computer. Another black screen appeared, and the familiar white text began to run across the screen.

"What are you doing?" asked Rupert.

"I thought you were done with the questions?" replied the man. His attitude had stiffened.

"I'll ask all the questions I like," said Rupert. He leaned forward to place the muzzle of the gun against the back of the man's head. "Now, tell me what you're doing."

"The hidden sensor is on a sub-system of the sensor network. If the first three sensors are disabled, the sub-system kicks in. I'm finding the IP address of the sub-system so I can then hack into it and disable it. If I don't do that, the alarms will go off as soon as the diamond is lifted from the cushion. It's a pressure sensor."

Rupert watched the commands he was entering and saw nothing untoward. Another browser opened, and the man entered the IP address of the sub-system. This time he entered the right password first time around.

A similar graphical representation of the building appeared, and the man flipped the building, zoomed and found the diamond display.

A single sensor floated in the air where the previous screen had shown three.

"That's it?" Rupert asked.

The man didn't reply. Instead, he hit the push to talk button on the mic.

"Secondary sensor is going down in three, two, one."

He clicked a button on the screen to disable the sensor; the icon turned red.

A few strokes of the keyboard and he switched back to the first screen then located the three sensors beneath the glass display.

"Primary sensors going down in ten seconds, but I can't keep them off for long before it's noticed. You've got about five seconds to lift the lid, grab what you need, and close the lid again."

"I'm ready," said the girl in response.

"Okay. Three, two, one."

CHAPTER TWENTY-SEVEN

Centuries of history stood silent and still before Harvey. He waited at the edge of the small alcove with the diamond and Melody behind him. Their own history was thick in the air, and the tension between them was electric.

"Harvey, I need your help here," said Melody.

He turned as she pushed the button on her ear-piece.

"I'm ready," she said to Reg. "Harvey, I need you to lift the edge of the glass when Reg gives the signal. I'll take the diamond."

Harvey stepped over to her, looked at the glass, then back at Melody. He pulled on a pair of thin cotton gloves and placed his hands either side of the display.

"Now."

Harvey raised the glass just enough for Melody to reach in and grab the diamond, which seemed to sparkle and glitter in response.

Harvey lowered the glass lid.

"It's down. We're good," said Melody to Reg, as she pocketed the diamond. "Now get us the hell out of here."

She listened to Reg's commands then gave Harvey a nod.

"Okay, we're leaving," said Melody, heading for the door to the service corridor. "How long do we have before the cameras come back on?"

She pulled open the door and stepped through into the walkway with Harvey right behind her. Immediately, two hands reached out and forced her to the floor. A guard stood over her, holding her arm behind her back. She'd hit her head in the fall; her body fell limp and her eyes closed. A small track of blood was smeared along the corridor wall.

Harvey sprang into action.

He swung the cosh, hard, fast and with violence. It connected with the back of the guard's head. His knees buckled, and he crumpled to the floor on top of Melody. Harvey pulled the guard off her and stole the man's radio. The channel was alive with crackled and frantic messages.

"They're on to us," said Harvey. "Come on, Melody. You need to wake up."

He rolled Melody onto her back and straightened her twisted arm. Without hesitation, Harvey reached down, removed her ear-piece and put it on his own ear before flicking the small switch that permanently opened the comms channel, eliminating the need for the wearer to push the button to communicate. He scooped Melody up in his arms and made towards the door.

"Reg, come back," said Harvey. He made his way along the corridor. "Reg?"

A familiar but timid voice came back in his ear. "Harvey? Is that you? What have you done with her?"

"No time, Reg," said Harvey. "She's down. I need an exit and fast."

"I'm just clearing the cameras."

"No time. We're blown. Get me out of here," said Harvey. "Fastest exit possible."

He shoved through the double doors just as two more guards reached the top of the stairs. Harvey kicked one directly in the chest sending him back down the hard steps. The other swung his cosh, but Harvey was faster. He twisted Melody out of the way and landed his forehead directly onto the man's nose.

The guard held his face with both hands. Harvey stamped down on his knee, bending his leg the wrong way, then stepped aside to allow the man to fall down howling like a baby with shrill screams that echoed through the stairwell.

"Fastest exit is the loading bay," said Reg.

"I had a feeling you were going to say that," said Harvey. "Can you meet me around the back?"

"Copy that," said Reg.

Three more guards heaved through the double doors as Harvey reached the bottom of the stairwell. One held a Taser pointed at Harvey, but all three hollered panicked commands at him to stop and get down on the floor.

"Easy, boys," Harvey replied. "Do you mind if I put her down first?"

Two of the men looked at the man in the middle, a middle-aged officer who stood tall and confident of his team's success.

"Do it slowly," he said. "Then lay on the floor beside her with your arms stretched out in front of you."

Harvey nodded as if submitting to his request. He bent and placed Melody on the cold, hard floor. Then, in an instant, he pulled Melody's Sig from his belt.

"Taser down now," said Harvey.

The three men all raised their hands in the air.

The Taser clattered to the floor at their feet.

"Kick it away," said Harvey.

The man closest to the weapon did as he was told.

"You, fat man," said Harvey, nodding at the large man who was closest to Harvey and holding out a bunch of zip ties. "Grab his wrist." Harvey gestured at the boss. "Tie it to the boy's wrist." Harvey gestured at the younger man on the end who had dropped the Taser.

The large man did as he was told.

"Now tie your own wrists to them both," said Harvey. He bent and collected Melody, keeping a firm hold on the handgun.

"Tight," he reminded them.

He heard the short, sharp zips of the ties being pulled tight.

"Good," said Harvey. "Nobody needed to get hurt, did they? Now sit down."

The three men sat down in unison as Harvey collected Melody from the floor and slipped through the double doors with her in his arms. She began to stir but was incoherent.

As Harvey entered the loading bay through the last set of doors, one more guard came at him. He was young and over-enthusiastic. Harvey heard his wild run up even before he saw him.

Harvey stopped.

Almost in disbelief, Harvey stared at the young man who was running full pelt at them both, readying to launch himself and take them to the floor. Their eyes met.

The guard carried on running.

Harvey didn't move.

Still running, the guard drew closer.

Harvey didn't look away.

The young guard suddenly lost momentum. His death cry waned to a murmur and then petered out to nothing.

Harvey glared at him.

The boy stood motionless in front of Harvey with his head hung low as if ashamed.

"Sit," said Harvey.

The boy dropped to a cross-legged position on the floor in front of Harvey.

Harvey kicked the single door open to the side of the loading bay, dropped down the small flight of concrete stairs, and walked calmly to Reg's waiting van.

Approaching sirens blared from all directions.

The van's side door slid open as he approached.

CHAPTER TWENTY-EIGHT

"Stop here," Rupert shouted.

The man had transferred from his place by the computers to the driver's seat to move the van.

"You won't get away with this," he replied with fresh confidence. "You don't know who's in there."

Rupert laughed. "My friend, I believe Harvey and I have spoken already. Interesting chap. Talented too, I hear."

"If you knew him, you wouldn't be waiting out here for him," said the man.

Rupert gave a soft laugh in the tense darkness of the van.

"He has quite the reputation, doesn't he?" he said. "Well, let's see how he deals with me."

"You'll need more than a gun to stop him."

"We'll see about that," said Rupert. He popped the magazine from the handgun, checked it and reloaded.

"What do you plan on doing with *us?*" the man asked.

Rupert watched for the single door of the loading bay to open through the tinted side window. Police sirens began to grow close and seemed to multiply the nearer they came.

"It's Reg, isn't it?" asked Rupert. "I heard him call you Reg."

"Yeah, it is," Reg replied.

"Well, Reg," said Rupert. "I have some ideas, and it all depends on how you and your friends react. Play nicely, and you might not get hurt, but mess me about, and you'll find that I have a sharp side. I can be quite playful." Rupert smiled as if to confirm his statement.

"He's coming," said Reg.

Rupert glanced out the window and saw a man carrying the girl in his arms. Rupert slid the side door open and stepped back with the gun raised. Harvey laid her down on the van's wooden floor and took a step up.

"Go, Reg," he said. "Don't hang about." He began to pull himself into the van.

"Not so fast, hero," said Rupert from the shadows.

Harvey froze.

"Come on guys. I can see the police," said Reg from the front of the van. "We're running out of time."

"Step down, Harvey," said Rupert.

"You're going to leave me here?" Harvey replied.

"Oh no, Harvey. This is the end for you, for what you did to Bob and Bill. But I wanted to look you in the eye before I killed you." Rupert offered his warmest smile again.

"Guys, can we discuss this on the way?" said Reg. His voice was racked with nerves, which were at their breaking point.

"Shut it," screamed Rupert. "Just shut your mouth and do as you're told."

He turned to back Harvey.

"You," he gestured at Harvey with the gun, waving it at his foot. "Off. Now."

Harvey slowly removed his foot from the van, his eyes never leaving Rupert's.

Rupert re-aimed the gun at Harvey's face. The two men shared a tense moment. The man didn't seem frightened at all.

If the girl he clearly cared about hadn't been lying at Rupert's feet, he would probably have jumped on him, a fact that Rupert made careful note of.

"Where's the diamond?" asked Rupert.

It was a few tense seconds before Harvey finally spoke.

"In my pocket. Why don't you come and take it off me?"

"Is that right?" said Rupert. He bent and ran his hands along Melody's pockets.

Rupert's grin grew into a laugh. He shook his head at his own luck as his hand closed around a golf ball-sized lump.

"Bad luck, Harvey," said Rupert. He stood, preparing to squeeze the trigger.

"Reg, *now*," said Harvey, and span out of sight.

Reg gunned the engine. The van lurched forward and Rupert lost his balance. He pulled a single shot, but it went wide into the air. Rupert clung to the side of the van, dragged himself upright, and then slammed the side door in anger.

"I didn't tell you to go," he screamed at the driver. "Turn back."

Reg cowered at the wheel.

"Turn around?" he asked. "We can't turn-"

Rupert kicked out at the chairs with fury. "Just drive, and don't do anything I don't tell you to do."

"Where am I going?" asked Reg, visibly scared. "There's police everywhere."

"To the river," said Rupert, as he fumbled through the girl's pockets. "Turn onto Queen's Gate and don't stop for lights."

Rupert searched through the girl's black hooded sweatshirt. His hand fell on something familiar. He reached in and pulled out the GPS tag that Glasgow George had fixed to her wrist. He tossed it aside then felt through the pockets of her black cargo pants where he'd felt the lump a few minutes earlier.

He slid two fingers into her pants pocket then slowly pulled out a perfect diamond the size of a golf ball and identical to the one he had stashed at Smokey's house.

It glittered in the soft light. The weight felt reassuring in his hand. He was mesmerised.

Reg swung the van hard to the left as he turned onto Queen's Gate. Two police cars screamed past in the opposite direction. Rupert held on tight with one hand, and holding the diamond up in the air, he closed his fist, kissed his newfound fortune, and pocketed it, tapping his pocket as if to confirm to himself that it was safe.

He felt his anger dissipate and a calm relief washed over him. "It's turned out to be a successful night, Mr Reg," said Rupert. "You get me to the boat, and you just might live after all."

CHAPTER TWENTY-NINE

The van pulled away and left Harvey standing outside the rear of the museum in the dead of night. Police sirens were growing louder. Flashing blue lights approached in front and to both sides of his peripheral vision. He remained still for a few more seconds, pinned to the ground as he watched the van turn onto Queen's Gate then disappear. Then Harvey jumped into action as if shaken from a dream.

He ran directly away from the museum along Museum Lane. His head pounded with anger, and his chest thumped at the loss of Melody. A police car pulled into the lane in front of him at high speed, blocking his exit.

The driver accelerated towards him.

Harvey didn't slow down, nor did he move to the side of the narrow road, which was blocked on either side by huge buildings. He could see the passenger's face prepare for a collision as the car grew nearer. Harvey ran faster, giving everything he had.

Then, at the last possible moment, the driver pulled the wheel to the left and pulled the handbrake up. The length of the car almost filled the width of the lane. Harvey jumped across the front of the car as the doors opened. He landed on his backside, slid off the car's polished surface onto the road, and was away.

"Stop. Armed police," yelled the passenger, who was closest to Harvey. The policeman gave chase and tried to grab onto Harvey's jacket but missed. Harvey pumped his arms as he ran. He sprinted towards the edge of the building, waiting for the shots to begin. He dived around the side of the Science Museum, which occupied the other side of Museum Lane, and stopped. Jumping back against the wall under a small copse of trees, he stopped and listened as the policeman's boots approached. At the first sign of the man appearing around the corner, Harvey whipped out the telescopic cosh, reached out from the shadows and swung it hard against the policeman's knees.

He fell to the grass in a silent whimper and rolled to a stop.

Harvey wasted no time. He heard the car turning behind him in the lane, and cut through the trees beside the Science Museum, then sprinted through an alleyway another hundred yards along the road. There, he found his motorbike parked beside two expensive-looking saloon cars, exactly where he'd left it.

Squealing tyres and brakes told Harvey that more police had arrived at the museum. The area was lit with flashing blue lights. Bouncing headlights in the alleyway behind Harvey showed that the other cop was hunting for him behind the Science Museum.

He pulled his helmet on quickly, started the bike, and rode casually away from the scene. Winding his way out of the back streets, he passed the Natural History Museum less than two minutes after Melody had been taken. At least twenty police cars had since blocked Museum Lane and they had begun to block the main road to the front of the building. He took a quick look at the scene before turning towards the river, where the van had disappeared at the junction of Queen's Gate.

Harvey waited until he was out of sight of the police then dropped into second gear with his sights firmly set on the river less than a mile directly ahead of him.

There was no need to brake or change gear on the bike once he hit one hundred and ten miles per hour. The roads were quiet, and he passed the few cars in a flash before they even knew he was approaching.

As the black strip of the river came into view, Harvey eased off the accelerator. At the entrance to the small dock, sitting with its doors wide open, was the van. Harvey approached carefully, but the van was empty.

The buildings on the far side of the river reflected lights of red, blue and yellow off the water's surface. By the time Harvey reached the water and had slowed to a stop beside the little dock, the lights were shimmering in the wake of a distant boat. Its waning portside light grew smaller and disappeared into the night.

Harvey stared after the boat heading south on the river. He was too late. A rage began to boil inside him.

He revved the bike's engine once. Then his anger got the better of him, popping in his mind like a pressure valve. With a hard twist of the throttle, the engine roared, screaming in revolt, but he held it, venting his anger and frustration through the engine. Then he slipped into first gear, popped the clutch and locked the front brake hard down. The rear wheel span on the cobbled road, sending the back of the bike in a slow circle. A cloud of tyre smoke filled the night around him. Once the bike had turned to face the way he'd came, he released the brake and roared up the street, his mind firmly set on South London.

CHAPTER THIRTY

A heavy stale smell of charred meat intertwined with an acrid, acidic odour clung to the back of Melody's throat. She gagged then dry-heaved but couldn't lean forward to spit. Instead, fiery saliva dribbled from her lips onto her lap.

A hood had been pulled over her head, which shut out any direct light and view of the room. But she felt strong heat and just faintly saw a glow of orange in front of her through the loose fabric of the hood. Everything else was dark.

Somewhere far off, in another room perhaps, Melody could hear the soprano section of an orchestra, though she couldn't make out the exact piece.

A desperate fight for life kicked in.

Melody was immediately aware that she was sitting down with her hands bound behind her and her ankles tied to the chair legs. She fought her restraints, pulling her arms and legs in all directions, but to no avail.

"Harvey?" she called, with a breathless, weak, dry rasp. "Is that you?"

No reply came for a few seconds until a slow, crying hinge

turned, like some wild animal's dying breath. It pierced the space around her, and the heat of the room intensified.

"Reg?" she called. The force of her voice on her dry throat scratched and sent her into a coughing fit. She spat blindly to rid her throat of the burning saliva.

"Melody?"

It was Reg's voice.

"Reg?" she wheezed. "Where are you?"

Reg didn't reply.

"Reg, talk to me," said Melody.

"I can't, Melody," said Reg, his voice high with emotion.

"Reg? Tell me what's wrong."

She could tell he was somewhere in front of her, but the hot glow was all she could vaguely see.

Reg sniffed once and sighed.

"Are you crying?" asked Melody. "Talk to me. We can get out of this, Reg."

"You'll be going nowhere fast, young lady," said a voice, cold and hard, with a twang of a Welsh accent.

Blind to her surroundings, the voice conjured an image in Melody's mind of a man in his fifties with a flock of silver hair above each ear and small spectacles resting gently on the bridge of a large nose.

"Who are you?" she asked. "Where am I?"

"You're in purgatory, dear," the voice replied. "Relax while your path is decided. You're on the cusp of heaven and hell. There's a tug of war happening between the devil and the big man himself."

His face suddenly blocked the glow of the fire. He almost whispered.

"And you're the prize."

"Who are you?" asked Melody.

The shape of the man's face moved away, and the orange

glow returned to the centre of Melody's view. With it came the dry heat that prickled every tiny hair on Melody's skin.

"That's an easy one," he replied. "I am the shepherd. *I* am the shining light which will guide your way, and I am your soulless chaperone from this world to the next."

"Reg, are you hearing this?"

"Silence," the voice spat. "The time for questions is over. Your friend is about to begin his own journey."

"Melody?" mumbled Reg.

"Reg?" cried Melody. *"Reg."*

A strong smell hit Melody's nose of chemicals, but not familiar.

"Reg?" Melody screamed.

The flat palm of a hand struck Melody hard across her face.

Then the hand returned to her cheek, but this time the touch was soft. His thumb reached into the hood and gently caressed her skin. She tried to move away, but her restraints held her there.

"Don't fight it," the man said.

His hand slid slowly to her neck. His body passed in front of her, once more revealing the orange glow like a beacon in the dark.

She felt him standing behind her. His hand was working its way along her collarbone, soft hands, but cold to the touch.

A small moan of relief issued from his throat as he inhaled the smell of Melody's hair. She pictured him standing behind her with his head tilted back, his face half lit by the glowing orange fire in front of where she sat.

His hand dropped further. His fingers found the top of her tight black t-shirt.

Melody's heart raced. Her breathing quickened. His hand slid across her clammy skin and found what he was looking for.

"Get your dirty hands away from me," Melody spat.

The man responded with a small groan and pushed himself into Melody's back. As much as she struggled, Melody couldn't get away from the push of his groin and the squeeze of his hand.

"Don't fight me, dear," he said. "I can make your journey easy." He gave a hard squeeze. "Or I can make it painful. The path you take is not my decision, but how I lead you there, well, you decide."

He slipped his hand out of her shirt and walked away. Melody felt his presence move around her like a shadow in the darkness. He began to hum to the soft music that played somewhere far off. She heard the metallic clangs and clatters of what sounded like tools being placed on a surgical trolley. It was followed by the gulp and gargle of a liquid container being turned upside down, like a water dispenser. Finally, Melody heard a small squeak of a tap or a valve and the roar of open flames growing louder.

A door opened behind Melody, allowing a cool breeze to enter the room. It sent a chill from Melody's ankles to her face, forming goosebumps that shuddered through to her very core.

"Doctor Feelmore," said a new authoritative voice from behind Melody. "Are we ready?"

CHAPTER THIRTY-ONE

With a tug of the thin material, the hood pulled away from the girl's head. Rupert tossed it into the glowing furnace behind him, which sat like a hungry beast at feeding time.

He watched as the girl blinked her eyes and squinted. Then, as her vision adjusted, she focused on his feet. Her head rose as she took him in, slowly letting her eyes fall onto Rupert's for the first time.

Rupert gave her time to look around the room as far as the restraints allowed. She gave a distasteful glare at Doctor Feelmore, who smiled like the creep that he was in return. Then her eyes fell on her friend who lay on the gurney.

The girl's face fell in dismay at the sight of him. A drip of embalming fluid was inserted into his arm, just waiting to be turned on, and a draining tray lay beneath his thigh.

It would be a painful death. The worst imaginable.

"How long does it take for a man to die like this, doctor?" asked Rupert. He fixed his gaze upon the girl.

"It will be interesting to find out, Mr Bond," replied the doctor. "I've never embalmed a *live* person before. But I would say seven or eight minutes. The acid will very quickly eat away at his veins and arteries, which will be excruciating. I would suggest then heart would give out before the loss of blood takes effect, through the pain, you understand. But we'll see."

Rupert glanced at the doctor, nodded his thanks for his professional opinion, and returned his stare to the girl.

"How's your head?" he asked.

She returned his stare with equal distaste.

"Fine," she said.

Rupert nodded at her friend on the gurney. "You love this man?"

"Like a brother," the girl replied.

Rupert allowed silence to ensue before speaking. He enjoyed seeing how people reacted under pressure.

"You understand what we're doing here, right?" he asked. "You can see the lengths we're going to in order to make you suffer."

"I can see," she replied. "But for the life of me, I can't understand why."

"Do you know who I am, Lola?" he asked.

She looked confused.

"No," she said. "No, I don't know who you are. I've never seen you before and my name is not-"

"Well, let me enlighten you," said Rupert, cutting her off before the conversation deviated from where he intended. "My name is Rupert Bond. You may have heard of me?"

"No. I can't say I have."

"Your friend Harvey has, Lola, and if I may jog your memory a little, you helped him burn the face off my good friend Mad Bob and cut the throat of Cannon Bill. I knew them both for many years, and they were very loyal men."

"I have absolutely no idea-"

"Don't interrupt me, Lola," said Rupert. Anger began to rise in his voice. "You and your friend Reg here, or should I call him

Fingers? Not only did you both help our friend Harvey kill my two good friends, but you have potentially damaged our reputation. I can't have the good people of South London running away with the idea that it's okay to knock off the Bond Brothers without a sniff of retribution or retaliation. Or punishment," Rupert finished.

"You've got the wrong-"

"You don't talk until I tell you to talk, Lola," snapped Rupert.

The girl let her head drop.

"So, I needed a way to make you suffer, and luckily for me, my good friend Doctor Feelmore here not only has the skills to prolong that suffering but as you can see, being a doctor of mortuary science, he also has the necessary tools to dispose of your bodies."

"You have the diamond. Let us go," said the girl.

"No," replied Rupert, cold and hard.

"Can I speak?" she asked.

Rupert nodded. "You can talk, but the only thing I want to hear from you is the word, sorry," said Rupert. "And *sir*," he added with finality.

"He'll find you."

"I doubt that," replied Rupert with a laugh.

"The harder you make this on me, the longer it'll take for you to die."

"Not very convincing."

"You've got to believe me. He won't give up. He'll find you and-"

And?" said Rupert. He held the back of her hair and pulled her head back in a swift, sharp movement. "That's just it, you see. I want him to find me. I want him to show his face because I'm going to tear it off."

She blinked away the pain.

"You don't know him," she said. "You don't know what he's capable of."

"Oh, no, no," said Rupert. "It is he who doesn't know what *I* am capable of."

The girl's expression dropped to a submissive tone of pity.

"Then do what you will," she said. "But believe me, you'll be sorry."

Rupert shoved her head away and put his face close to hers.

"I'll look forward to it, sweetheart."

Rupert's pocket began to vibrate.

"Think about your next words, Lola," he said as he straightened. "They'll be the last ones Reggie over there ever hears."

Rupert pulled his phone from his pocket, recognised the number and hit the connect button.

"Smokey," he said. "I wondered when I'd hear from you."

CHAPTER THIRTY-TWO

The thin wooden door of the little houseboat was no match for Harvey's heavy boot. It swung back and smashed against the tiny kitchenette, breaking free from its top hinge. It rocked back and forth for a moment, then crashed to the floor.

Harvey ducked inside the cabin and stood tall over Fingers, who had frozen at the sound of the crashing front door. Fingers stood poised with the bundle of rolled up drawings in his arms and a small holdall on the floor beside him.

"Going somewhere, Fingers?" asked Harvey.

"Oh, thank God it's you," said Fingers. "I thought they'd come for me."

"Who?" said Harvey. "Who would have come for you?"

"The Bond Brothers," whispered Fingers. His eyes darted to the narrow view of the canal's towpath through the side window.

"There's no-one out there," said Harvey.

"Are you sure? I heard the police helicopter go over a while ago."

"You're the geek, right?" asked Harvey.

Fingers responded with a confused look.

"The geek, the computer guy," said Harvey. "You're the one that gets Lola inside so she can do her job. Am I right?"

Fingers nodded.

Harvey took a step forward.

"Find me Lola," said Harvey.

Fingers took a step backwards.

"I don't know where she is," said Fingers. "You saw yourself; she was thrown into the back of that van."

"Find me the tag she was wearing."

Harvey held his gaze.

"She dropped it," said Fingers. "I saw it fall."

"I picked it up," said Harvey, "after you drove off and left me there."

Fingers lowered his eyes to the floor. "I was scared," he said. "I didn't know what to do."

"Sit down," said Harvey.

Fingers remained standing, open mouthed and staring at the floor.

With a single sweep of his arm, Harvey cleared the small dining table that stood between the two men.

"I said sit down," he shouted.

Fingers dropped back onto the small U-shaped couch, still clutching the rolls of building plans to his chest.

Harvey collected the holdall from where it sat on the floor, unzipped the zipper, and tipped the bag upside down. The contents scattered across the old rug that covered the boat's polished wooden floor. Some paperwork, a passport, a few items of clothing and a laptop lay in a heap. Harvey bent and picked up the laptop. He tossed it at Fingers, who dropped the rolls of paper and caught it as if it were the most precious thing he owned.

"Find the tag."

"What tag?" asked Fingers, stalling. "I don't know how to find it."

Harvey didn't reply.

With an air of reluctance, Fingers set the laptop down on the table, opened it and began to type.

Harvey moved around the tiny room to see the screen.

Fingers edged away.

"You're afraid of me?" Harvey asked.

"With all due respect, sir, I watched you set fire to a man's face and cut another man's throat," said Fingers. "It's fair to say I'm a little wary of you."

Fingers' fingers danced across the keys in short spurts. Harvey noticed how they moved in fits then hovered as his eyes scanned a line of text, and then burst into life again. The movements reminded Harvey of Reg; he used to do exactly the same thing.

"That's why they call you Fingers then, is it?" said Harvey.

Fingers kept his eyes on the laptop screen and issued a quiet, "Mm-hmm." It was exactly how Reg used to sound when he was focused on something.

"Okay," said Fingers. "I'm into the GeoTech Tracking Platform. There's about six hundred live tags in the London area. I have no way of knowing which is Lola's."

"Seven, four, five, six," began Harvey. "Six, eight, two, five, nine, three, four."

"You memorised the serial number?" said Fingers, clearly impressed. He tapped the number that Harvey recalled into the search function.

"Have you found it?" asked Harvey.

Fingers sucked in a lungful of air through his teeth and let it out with a long hiss.

"The Crematorium of Greater South London," said Fingers, spinning the laptop around for Harvey to see a little icon on a map. It hovered over a patch of green in the middle of what was clearly residential streets.

Harvey zoomed the map out, fixed the location in his mind then shut the laptop. He reached up to the window, opened it a little, and tossed the laptop out. It landed with a splash in the canal below.

"You just..." began Fingers. "That was my..."

Harvey glared at him.

"So you're *leaving* now?" asked Fingers, with hope in his voice.

Harvey sighed then leaned on the couch opposite Fingers.

"What's your real name, Fingers?"

"Jeremy, sir."

"Jeremy what?"

"Jeremy Hawes," replied Fingers. His voice quavered, and his eyes were wide open as if they'd been glued.

"Mind if I call you Fingers?" asked Harvey.

Fingers shook his head.

"Good. So is there something you want to tell me?" asked Harvey. "And before you feed me a pack of lies, you should know that I'm extremely good at knowing when somebody is telling the truth." Harvey pulled his knife from the sheath sewn into the inside of his jacket. "And I know when they're playing me for a fool," he finished.

He turned the knife in his hands, feeling the familiar texture of the wood. It was the same knife his mentor had given him when he was a teenager, and the same knife Harvey had used to extract the truth from many men of all shapes and sizes.

"I'm waiting," said Harvey.

"It was her idea," said Fingers. "I just helped." He gestured at the empty space where the laptop had been.

Harvey didn't reply. He raised an eyebrow.

"The diamond was all she thought about," said Fingers. His

head dropped in defeat. "She said it belonged to her. It was rightfully hers."

"Lola LaRoux," said Harvey.

"Exactly. You know the story? It belonged to her family or something. I don't know. But they've been after it for years and when-"

"Yeah, yeah," said Harvey. "When the diamond was spotted, she convinced you and the other fella-"

"Dynamite," interjected Fingers.

"She convinced you and Dynamite to rob it?"

"That's right. It was all her idea. I just-"

"Helped?" asked Harvey.

"Yeah, I just helped. We knew each other from way back. I went to school with Dynamite, we did a few jobs years ago."

"Something doesn't add up," said Harvey. "I'm a simple man, Fingers. To me, everything is either black or it's white. It either is or it isn't. I don't believe in God. But I would never disrespect someone who does, you understand? That's their choice. Do you see a picture of who I really am?"

"A simple man," said Fingers. "Black or white. Yeah, I understand."

"Good," continued Harvey. "Can you tell me the story about when the brothers put the tag on Lola?"

"The wrist tag?" said Fingers. His eyes somehow grew larger as if he could sense where Harvey was taking the conversation. "We did a job."

"Tell it like it is, Fingers," interrupted Harvey. "You stole the missing diamond."

Fingers nodded.

"Yeah, we did. We stole the missing diamond. But when Lola and Dynamite went in, the Bond Brothers found me in the van hidden in the trees. So when Lola and Dynamite came running from the job, they shot Dynamite and put the tag on Lola. That's when they told her to rob the second diamond."

"And if she didn't rob the second diamond, they'd kill you both?"

Fingers nodded. "And our families."

Harvey began to pace the few short steps from the small dining table to the broken front door, and back.

"So, who took Lola then?" asked Harvey. "Who threw her in the van the other day?"

"I don't know," said Fingers. "It all happened so quick."

"Yeah, I saw it. One minute you were both there, the next she was in the back of the van, and it was tearing off down the road. I saw it all, you know, Fingers?"

Fingers held his gaze. His eyes had begun to shine with the inevitable tears that would come soon.

"Did you see me?" asked Harvey. "Did you see me there, Fingers?"

Fingers nodded. It was almost indiscernible, but it was a nod.

"You saw me, and you just drove off. And don't tell me you were scared."

Fingers stayed silent.

"You see, that's another thing I can't understand. Why would someone drive off in the opposite direction so quickly after their friend had just been kidnapped?"

Fingers looked at the floor.

"And why, if they took Lola, would they not take you as well?" asked Harvey. "You're a witness, right?"

Silence.

"And this is the big one, Fingers. Why, if they found you at the first robbery, did they not either shoot you or put a tag on you?"

"I guess they didn't need-"

"Didn't need to?"

Fingers began to cry. Silent tears fell from his cheeks to the old rug that lay beneath the table.

"It's not me they want, is it? They want Lola. She's got the skills they need. She's the one who can break into places, not me."

"So you set Lola up? *You* had her kidnapped?" said Harvey. "You also set me up. You *knew* that I'd go and get the diamond, didn't you?"

Fingers nodded.

"And now, two of my good friends are in trouble, Fingers, and the Bond Brothers still have the diamond."

A loud sob announced the arrival of a full confession. The waters broke. Fingers crumpled into a folded mess on the couch. He drew his knees to his chest and buried his head between his legs.

Harvey stepped out through the broken door and reached for a fuel can he'd seen resting on the prow of the boat. He stepped back inside, unscrewed the lid and tossed it to one side.

Fingers' eyes lit up with horror.

"I did it to save her," whined Fingers. "You have to understand. Her father knows some men. I told him she was in trouble and we made a plan. He helped me."

Harvey waited for the rest of the story. He'd seen it a hundred times. The confessor usually felt glad to finally tell someone their secret. Once they started, the whole story came out.

He began to douse the furniture in petrol while he waited for Fingers to open up.

"If Lola got the diamond, I knew they'd still kill her and probably me as well."

"I'm listening."

"And if we didn't get the diamond, then they'd still kill us both. But if we gave them you-"

"Right," said Harvey. "So are you saying you had Lola kidnapped because you knew that I'd go in and rob the diamond anyway?"

"I'm sorry. You were the only one capable of getting away. If I let Lola do the robbery, she'd have got the diamond for sure. But they'd of killed her anyway, just like they did Dynamite. It was the only way to save her," said Fingers.

"But what about if I killed you?"

Fingers shrugged and stared at the floor.

"I'm dead anyway, let's face it. I didn't know what else to do," said Fingers.

He looked up. His eyes glowed red and snot ran from his nose in a stringy gloop. He looked wretched and simply stared at the floor.

Harvey placed the empty fuel can on the table with a loud thud like a drum. He kicked the passport on the floor over to Fingers' feet.

Fingers saw the movement. He reached down and picked it up, but looked at Harvey with confusion on his face.

"You're letting me go?" he asked.

Harvey didn't reply. Instead, he stuffed a wad of unopened letters into the toaster, which sat surrounded by breadcrumbs on the surface of the kitchenette. He pulled down the lever and set the timer to max, then turned the gas hob onto full.

Fingers jumped to his feet, scrambled over the drawings and his belongings to the door, and disappeared onto the footpath. Harvey gave the boat a cursory glance. Once he was happy that all the evidence would be burned, he stepped out to find Fingers, who was cowering behind a tree on the towpath fifty yards away.

"What have you done?" called Fingers, as Harvey causally approached him. "That's my boat."

A loud click cut through the night as the toaster popped up, followed by the rush of gases expanding, igniting, and seeking pockets of oxygen to burn, which combined in a whooshing ball of flame that mushroomed in the night sky.

The wooden hull of the boat exploded, sending shards of wood high into the air, which landed in the trees and grass behind Harvey.

"*Was* your boat," said Harvey, without turning back. "You just died in a very nasty explosion, Fingers. I suggest you get on the next plane out of here."

CHAPTER-THIRTY-THREE

"Charlie," called Rupert from the door. "Where are you?"

"Here," said another voice from somewhere further down the corridor.

"Well, get your arse in here," said Rupert, stepping back into the room.

He snatched the bag off Melody's head, but there was no painful stab of light in her eyes. The room was dark with just the dull glow of the furnace flames. The heat from the fire prickled her skin.

She stared up at Rupert, who stared back with the smug grin of someone who'd won, as his identical brother stepped into the room.

"Charlie, get Glasgow ready. We're going to the factory," said Rupert. "What were you doing out there anyway?"

"Not a lot."

Melody looked around once more and noticed they were in a chapel behind a large curtain. The cool breeze on her ankles came from the curtain. It was a crematorium.

"What were you doing, Charlie?"

"Looking at the bodies," he replied. "They're quite fascinating."

A broad grin ran across Doctor Feelmore's unashamed face.

"They're what? They're dead bodies," said Rupert. "You aren't supposed to be fascinated by them."

"What factory?" asked Charlie, ignoring his brother's distaste. "And what for?"

Rupert shook his head. "I just got a call. Smokey the Jew wants to meet us there for the handover."

"In a factory?"

"Yes," said Rupert.

"You mean the one where-"

"Mad Bob and Cannon Bill were killed? The very one," said Rupert.

"Can't we meet at a bar or something? Somewhere a bit nicer. I just had my shoes cleaned."

"When we're done, Charlie, you'll be able to buy a new pair every time you get one pair dirty. Now, I'm going to finish up here, you go get Glasgow George ready with the van."

"The van?" said Charlie. "It gets bloody worse. Why don't we go in the Bentley?"

"Are you going to question my every decision tonight, Charlie? Or can we crack on with this?"

"Alright, alright," said Charlie. "So who's that then?"

"Who's what?"

"Her?" said Charlie, nodding at Melody.

"That's Lola, you idiot. Who do you think it is?"

"Aren't we going to stay and watch the fun?"

"Charlie, you've got problems, you have," said Rupert. "We're about thirty minutes away from being richer than you can imagine, and you want to stay and watch this lot get burned alive?"

Charlie smiled at the comment.

"For Mad Bob," he replied. "And Bill."

"Charlie, we're leaving in five minutes. Get Glasgow ready."

Charlie huffed and left the room, muttering to himself. Rupert turned to Melody. He lowered himself down in front of her and spoke slowly and clearly.

"You, sweetheart, are a very stupid girl. You could have had it all."

Melody stayed silent.

"Doctor, do we, or do we not, pay extremely well?"

"Oh yes," said the doctor. "Very handsomely, I'd say."

"And how long have you worked for me, doctor?"

Melody began to hate the smug confidence with which the man spoke. His tailored suit, Italian shoes and well-groomed face were results of everything she opposed.

"Oh, about ten years, I'd say," replied the doctor. "Give or take."

"And, in that time, have either myself or my brother spoken to you with anything other than the highest respect?"

"Oh no, sir," the doctor replied. "Always a pleasure, it is."

"Did you hear that, Lola?" asked Rupert. "*Sir*."

He eyed her up and down. His lip curled and he spat in her face.

"You don't come to South London and mug off the Bond Brothers, sweetheart. When the good doctor here is done with you, your ashes will go in the toilet, and you should count yourself lucky. Mad Bob and Cannon Bill worked with us for a very long time, and you know, every single man that works for us would have quite gladly paid you a visit here to make your last few hours that little more..."

He flicked at Melody's chin to lift her head.

"Unbearable," he finished.

"So why don't they?" she asked.

"We, as it happens, Lola, we have a more pressing night ahead of us, and thanks to you, we'll be moving on to bigger and better things. So, you know, plans to make, people to see. But not to worry, of all the men that work for me, I'm certain the good doctor here is capable of making sure that my friends Bob and Bill are remembered."

He leaned forward and whispered into her ear.

"He's a sick man, and having a girl with a pulse will be a real treat for him, especially one as pretty as you."

Melody closed her eyes to block out the thoughts.

"Isn't that right, doctor?" said Rupert aloud.

"A pulse, why yes, sir," the doctor replied. "That'll make a nice change."

Rupert stared down at Melody. "See what I mean?" He stood to leave. From the doorway, he turned and spoke once more. "I'll leave you in the capable hands of our friend Doctor Feelmore, Lola."

Melody didn't reply.

"Doctor?" said Rupert.

"Sir?" the Doctor replied from his place in the corner.

The tiniest of moments hung between the sentences, but it was enough time for Melody to hear the music and picture Harvey and her on the beach near their farmhouse.

"Do your worst," said Rupert. "And make sure she suffers."

CHAPTER THIRTY-FOUR

Rain pelted the van as the three men journeyed the short distance through the South London suburb. Glasgow George drove the van. Charlie sat in the middle. Rupert was in the passenger seat.

"We're close, Rupert," said Charlie. "So bloody close. I can almost taste the sangria now. Why do you think he wants to meet here?"

"I don't know, Charlie, probably because he doesn't want the likes of us at his nice house."

"Well, what did Smokey actually say?"

"He said to meet him at Mad Bob's factory," said Rupert. "The instructions are quite clear, Charlie."

"Yeah but how did Smokey *know* that Mad Bob was killed there?" asked Charlie.

"Because it was his men that came and cleaned up the mess," said Rupert. "You don't think I'd have sent one of our own guys to clean up their mates' bod-"

Rupert stopped, aware that Glasgow was listening.

"That's what mates do, Charlie. When they lose a friend, they help out. Smokey's family and the Bonds go way back.

They've been wasting their money on art and big houses, while you and I, brother, have built a bloody empire."

"You put too much trust in that man, Rupert," said Charlie.

Rupert ignored his brother's lack of foresight and spoke directly to Glasgow. He was a stocky man, short, but fierce looking.

"Are you carrying, Glasgow?" asked Rupert.

Glasgow tapped the breast of his jacket where his handgun sat in its holster.

"Always, boss," he replied.

"You're a man of few words, Glasgow," said Rupert. "But tell me something. If this all works out how it should, Charlie and I will be shutting up shop here in London. We'll have enough money to retire. I think we've earned the chance to see out our mature years in the warmth and comfort of warmer climates-"

"And the warmth and comfort of several semi-naked women," said Charlie.

"So, Glasgow, tell us what you're going to do if we fold all this up?" continued Rupert, once more ignoring his brother.

Glasgow George's eyes didn't leave the road in front. His brow didn't furrow. His face remained impassive.

"What are my options?" he replied.

"Your options?" said Rupert. "That's a very level-headed question, Glasgow. So I'll give it to you straight. But remember this before you make up your mind. There is one more job you need to do for us in order to earn whatever you decide."

Glasgow nodded.

"The first option, Glasgow, is for you to take over here."

"Run the firm?" asked Glasgow.

"You've worked for us a very long time, and I've given the options an appropriate amount of consideration. If anyone was to take over, you're the only man I can see pulling it off. It'll be all yours, Glasgow. Naturally, you'd buy the assets from us at mates rates, and we can work out some kind of payment plan. But other than that, it'll be yours to run as you see fit."

Glasgow nodded once more.

"Option two. You carry on working for us. You come with us to wherever we decide to go and resume your role as head of security."

Glasgow, as ever, showed no preference to either.

"You'll be well paid, Glasgow," said Rupert, as a sweetener.

"What's the job?" asked Glasgow. "You said there was one last job."

Rupert considered how best to sell the idea to a man as ruthless, yet simple, as Glasgow.

"As I recall," he began, "Mad Bob and Cannon Bill were mates of yours, were they not?"

Glasgow's mouth turned into a grimace. Rupert watched at the effect the two men's names had on the man.

"They meant a lot to us too, Glasgow. They worked for us for a very long time and helped us build the empire we now enjoy. I wondered what it might feel like for those of us who knew Bob and Bill so well to get our hands on the man that killed them."

Glasgow nodded.

"Is he coming?" asked George.

"He is, Glasgow. He's coming right for us."

Glasgow's face seemed to bunch up in the dim light. It was difficult to tell if the expression was of hate, pain, or perhaps a smile.

"One last act to close off this whole episode, George, and to allow them the rest they deserve. What do you say to that?"

"You want me to kill him?" asked George.

"Oh no, Glasgow," said Rupert with a grin. "I want you to *catch* him. I want him caught, so that we can all take turns in killing him. We're going to kill the fucker so many times he's going to wish he'd never set foot in London. He's going to wish he'd never been born, Glasgow."

Glasgow nodded once more. The silhouette of his huge face rocked twice against the driver side window.

"You don't have to make a decision now, George, about if you'd prefer option one or option two. But I have a feeling that the chance to complete your little mission might come tonight, and if it does, I want you to be ready."

"So you reckon he'll definitely come, Rupert?" asked Charlie. "This Harvey bloke?"

"He'll be here alright," said Rupert, "and we'll close this little episode off once and for all."

Glasgow George stopped the van in the little lane outside the old factory. A chain-link fence secured the perimeter, and trees grew wild in the scrubland that bordered the lane and the building. The scene was empty of cars, people and movement, except the howling wind that tore at the treetops and sent the rain down diagonally.

"How do we get in, George?" asked Rupert.

"There's a hole in the fence over there," replied Glasgow, gesturing with a nod of his head.

"Good. Charlie, you come with me. Glasgow?" Glasgow George looked across at Rupert, his face as serious as it could be. "Go find our man Harvey."

"We're going to get soaked," said Charlie.

"No bruv," replied Rupert. "Tonight, we're going to get even, and we're going to get very bloody rich."

CHAPTER THIRTY-FIVE

The touch of Doctor Feelmore's hand against Melody's shoulder made her skin crawl. He'd closed the door behind the Bond Brothers and stood directly behind her.

The flames continued to burn inside the cremator but on a low setting as if they were only to warm the room and keep the furnace alight.

Reg had passed out on the conveyor belt.

"Just you and me then," said Feelmore. "I told you we'd have plenty of time to enjoy ourselves."

"Is this how you get your kicks?" said Melody. "You're a seriously disturbed man."

Feelmore reached down to Melody's chest, took a deep breath and groaned.

"So warm," he said. "My guests are usually much colder, you know?"

Melody struggled against the restraints. She was sure she could overpower him. She was held tight, but if an opportunity presented itself, she'd need to be ready to take it.

Feelmore laughed. "And they don't usually struggle so much. In fact, they rarely complain at all."

He slipped his hand from Melody's shirt and rested it on top of her head.

"I must say, you're a real treat," said Feelmore. "In addition to the warmth of your skin and the youth of your face, it's an absolute delight that you're so..." He searched for the words. "Alive with spirit," he finished. "I rarely get to sample one of your kind."

"My kind?" said Melody. "Do you have many guests?"

"Not so young, and hardly ever as pretty. But more importantly, you have a debt to pay," said Feelmore. "And for once I get to have you all to myself. I was once lucky enough to have the company of a female magistrate, who by chance or good fortune had recently brought the hammer down on some of the brothers' men. It was armed robbery or something, in the early days before they bought the clubs and bars."

Feelmore walked away from the chair. Melody couldn't see where he went but could hear his breathing close behind her.

A rustle of clothing.

He was undressing.

"Of course," continued Feelmore, "the boys all took delight in seeing her dead on my gurney one night. A few stayed for the after party. Not the brothers, no, they wouldn't get involved in that type of thing. But some of their boys would. And did."

A rattle of a belt broke the silence between Feelmore's rambling. Melody closed her eyes and thought of Harvey.

She thought of all the times she'd been in danger. It wasn't the first time she'd been caught, tied up and threatened. But for the first time, she could truly see no way out.

"The brothers turn a blind eye. They know what happens here. It doesn't make someone a bad person, you know? One bloke, in particular, Bill his name was, that's right, Cannon Bill, he came here often and paid well to get his kicks."

As much as Melody tried to picture Harvey, their farmhouse in France, and the life they had shared however briefly, she couldn't shake the image of Doctor Feelmore standing naked behind her with his face upturned as he recalled times of old.

"He was a quiet one, old Bill. Nice guy, don't get me wrong. Just quiet. You couldn't read him. Do you know what I mean, Lola? He was as hard as nails, built like a bleeding house with hands like shovels."

He rested his hands on Melody's shoulders from behind.

"Then he deserved what he got," spat Melody.

"I don't care what he did, but Bill didn't deserve to die like that. He didn't even need to be brought here. Apparently, they just scooped the bodies up with a shovel."

He moved away again. But this time, he stepped to the side of Melody and moved around in front of her, proud and smiling with the confidence of a child.

"It's strange, isn't it?" he said.

Melody let his words hang in the air a while, then fixed his gaze.

"What's strange, doctor?" she asked, her voice almost a whisper.

Feelmore looked down at Melody with curiosity and answered in a whisper equal to her own, but riddled in spite.

"How a man can be almost forgotten, a distant memory tucked somewhere in the far corners of your mind, until one day, the memory is recalled for some reason far removed from its purpose. Then the person is once again alive in your mind. But, as if to solidify the thought, that same person arrives in your life by virtue of an altogether separate interaction with somebody in another circle of life. Synchronicity, I believe they call it."

Melody opened her mouth to reply, but before the words found her voice, a distant sound, familiar and warm, brought hope to her heart.

A descending arpeggio of piano notes indicated the initial

bars of Beethoven's Moonlight Sonata. It was her father's favourite piece of music.

The music rose in volume from the speakers mounted high in the ceiling and beyond the curtains to Melody's side.

Feelmore looked around and up at the speakers.

The lights went out.

"I'd call it retribution," replied Melody.

Shadows danced on the walls of the chapel.

"Who's there?" called Feelmore.

But there was no reply, just a reassuring cool breeze that seemed to flow beneath the curtains and shake the furnace flames.

"I said who's there?" called Feelmore once again. "Announce yourself."

The curtain twitched to one side. Feelmore's head snatched at the movement. He grabbed a scalpel on the tray of surgical tools and stepped away behind Melody.

Melody closed her eyes and waited.

"I'm armed," called Feelmore. His bare feet scuffed the worn carpet as he edged away and his breathing quickened. "Show yourself or-"

His sentence was cut off with a gurgle. Then a loud sob left his lips. It was the type of involuntary cry that comes from the mind.

Melody heard Feelmore drop to the floor. He began to drag himself along the carpet, each movement accompanied by a soft pain-filled whimper. He turned himself and wrapped his arms around Melody's legs as if she would save him.

Feelmore was suddenly ripped away. He gave a cry like that of a child, which merged into long, painful sobs.

Melody strived to turn in her seat to see what was happening, but her restraints held her fast.

A few short moments of silence followed. Then Feelmore's

body slammed down onto the conveyor belt with a bang that sounded around the large room beyond the curtains.

A dark shape moved in front of the orange glow.

Melody hesitated then spoke softly. "Harvey?"

A long silence filled the room, but Melody felt his presence. She felt his security.

"Where are they?" asked Harvey.

"Who?" replied Melody. "The brothers?"

Harvey didn't reply.

"Some factory, I heard one of them say. But, Harvey, leave them. Forget it. We can move on."

Doctor Feelmore sniffed. He was crying like a child, Melody thought. How apt.

Harvey moved away from the whimpering man and stepped into the shadows. "The canal?" he said.

"I don't know. Something about Mad Bob's factory."

"It's the canal," said Harvey.

The dark shape of Doctor Feelmore was black against the glow of the furnace. From where Melody sat, she could see the knife that still stuck in the top of his spine, tall and erect.

Proud.

It was a wound Harvey had used before to disable the enemy, but prolong their life long enough for them to suffer.

"Is Reg okay?" asked Harvey.

"He's fine, just drugged I think."

"Are you okay? Did he hurt you?"

Harvey's hand rested on her shoulder as Feelmore's had, but it was warmer and stronger.

"Harvey, don't-"

"Did he hurt you, Melody?"

She took a deep breath and let it out slowly.

"No," said Melody. "You came in time."

"And if I hadn't?"

Melody couldn't bring herself to say the words.

Suddenly, the conveyor clunked into life. Its tiny gears worked themselves up to speed and the black shape of the doctor began its slow journey into hell.

"No," said Feelmore. "Stop, I tell you. I can explain."

He tried to roll away, but even from where Melody sat, she could see his limp body edge closer to the fire. His useless arms flailed, searching for something to hold onto, but they found nothing.

Melody felt a tug on her wrist ties.

"I'm going to cut your arms free," said Harvey. "You'll have time to untie your ankles and save him. Or you can watch him burn."

Feelmore's feet were inside the furnace. He gave a wild scream as the flames found his bare feet. His skin began to blister and smoulder.

"Harvey, no. Stop it. Stop the belt."

Harvey didn't reply.

"Harvey?" called Melody. "Harvey?"

A breath of cool air licked at Melody's ankles but it was quickly quashed by the heat from the fiery furnace.

Melody reached down and pulled at the loose ends of the rope that bound her ankles. She glanced up at Feelmore who was inside up to his knees and crying with the pitch of a soprano. His voice was hoarse from screaming, and sheer terror was carved on his face. His neck twisted to one side to see Melody.

"Help me," he croaked.

Melody stood from the chair and leapt to the big red button.

Her hand hovered over it.

She stared at the man on the belt as his waist began to disappear. Only his arms and head moved. His head rolled from one side to the other, and his hands beat down on the conveyor as if they were trying to beat it to a stop.

But the belt rolled on.

And the fire began to scorch his chest.

Feelmore had stopped moving by the time the furnace had fully consumed him. Maybe his heart had given up. Maybe his organs had failed. Or maybe his blood had boiled.

Melody wasn't sure of the exact cause of death, but she'd been enthralled by the spectacle, unable to remove her eyes from Feelmore's journey to hell.

Melody hit the stop button then turned the valve on the side of the furnace until the gas shut off. The orange glow fell to reveal a darkness and a silence. Just the ticking of the cooling metal and the popping and crackling of Feelmore's baked body could be heard.

A voice broke the silence, innocent like that of a child, but with the depth and wisdom of a man.

"Melody?" said Reg. "Are you there?"

Melody composed herself, took a few breaths, and then spoke.

"Reg, you're okay?"

"A little groggy. What happened?"

"It's over," she replied. "We're getting out of here."

Reg groaned and lay his head back down.

"Where are we going?"

Melody considered the various options. But there was only really one.

"We're going to get the devil twins, Reg."

CHAPTER THIRTY-SIX

Four large oil drums had been pulled into the centre of the huge, empty factory floor, twenty meters apart to form a square. The drums themselves had been filled with wood and petrol. The fires cast an orange light across the vast expanse of space.

A thick odour of petrol hung in the air from the oil drums. It mixed with the age-old grease and damp of the night.

Somewhere far off, a thunderstorm rolled by. Wind-swept rain hammered on the roof and the skylights of the old Victorian building like waves on a beach. They pelted the huge arched windows with millions of tiny *tap taps* as if a swarm of insects were fighting to get inside and escape the rain.

In the centre of the square of oil drums, standing with his hands tucked into the pockets of his long overcoat and facing the only open door, was Smokey the Jew. He stood alone and seemingly unafraid of the Bond Brothers. In front of him was one more oil drum, empty and upturned.

Lola LaRoux stood in the shadows of the first small office space, close to the pile of random boxes and machine parts that had been left behind by the last tenant. From where she stood, she had a clear view of the factory floor and the single doorway.

The two brothers eventually stepped into the room. The first stopped, shook his jacket, and then looked around before his eyes finally landed on Smokey. The second walked in close behind the first, ran his hands through his short hair and immediately saw Smokey.

They approached him side by side and entered the square, stopping a few meters before him with the upturned drum between them.

"My boys," said Smokey. "It's a nice night for it."

"Smokey," said Rupert in greeting. "How have you been?"

"I can't complain, Rupert," Smokey replied. "In fact, if the sun was shining out there and I was sitting by a pool drinking cocktails, life would be perfect."

"But it isn't perfect, is it Smokey?"

"No, Rupert. But we do our best, don't we? We make of it what we will."

"We do," said Rupert. "And lately we seem to have made quite a lot of it."

"You've certainly done well, boys. That you have."

"So where's the diamond?" said Charlie. "Did you bring it?"

"Ah, Charlie," said Smokey. "You always were the hasty one, weren't you?"

Rupert held his hand up to Charlie to quieten his brother.

"It's a fair question, Smokey," he said. "Did you bring it?"

Smokey lifted his hat and ran his fingers through his long hair.

"I did, Rupert," said Smokey. "But before I simply hand you your fortune, and as long-standing friends, I was wondering if you could tell me something."

"What?" said Charlie. "Why don't you just hand it over?" He turned to Rupert. "I told you we can't trust him."

"Rupert, I suggest you keep your dog on a leash, and might I remind you that you both put me in a very serious position when you asked me to look after the diamond. But I asked no questions, did I?"

"No, Smokey," said Rupert.

"I told no lies?"

"No, Smokey."

"So perhaps you could afford me a little respect and credibility before you attempt to tarnish my impeccable reputation with your slander, young Charlie."

Charlie didn't reply, but Smokey continued anyway.

"Before I begin, and to appease young Charlie here, let's see them both in all their glory."

The brothers looked at each other, then back at Smokey, who had pulled from his pocket two silk handkerchiefs, black, with the initials SA embroidered in gold thread in one corner.

He stepped forward and, keeping one hand in the pocket of his three quarter length overcoat, laid the two silk handkerchiefs down side by side on top of the upturned oil drum.

CHAPTER THIRTY-SEVEN

The he turned a watchful eye on the brothers as his hand felt inside his coat. With no more grace than if he was reaching for an apple, he pulled out the diamond and placed it on one of the handkerchiefs.

Smokey the Jew stepped away from the diamond, returned his hand to his pocket, and glanced from brother to brother.

"Your turn," he said.

Rupert dug into the pocket of his suit.

"What are you doing?" asked Charlie. He put his hand on Rupert's arm. "Just take the diamond and let's go."

Smokey observed the dynamics of the pair with keen eyes.

Rupert stepped forward and placed the second diamond on the second handkerchief beside its twin.

The three men stared in awe at the two rocks between them. Thunder grumbled its way closer, and the rain fell heavily onto the roof.

"Are you both aware of the story of the diamonds? Or to be more accurate, Demonios Gemolus?" said Smokey, breaking the silence.

"There's two of them," said Rupert. "They were split up years ago and have never been together since."

A deafening crash of thunder split the sky outside.

Charlie flinched at the noise. Rupert held Smokey's gaze.

"Do you know why they haven't been together since, Rupert?"

Rupert shook his head.

"No," he replied. "No, I don't."

"Would you like me to tell you?" asked Smokey. "I think you should know."

"Oh, this is bullshit," said Charlie. "Just hand-"

"Charlie, shut up," snapped Rupert. "I want to hear the story."

Charlie stuffed his hands in his pockets and looked away from them both.

"If you were twice as smart, Charlie, you'd be an idiot, you know that?" said Smokey.

"What's that supposed to mean? Charlie replied.

Smokey offered him a pitiful grin.

"It's just a saying we have," he replied. "Just a saying."

Smokey returned his attention to Rupert.

"The story goes, Rupert," he began, "that the diamonds were found in the years of Queen Victoria, somewhere in the arse end of what is now South Africa. They were found by a Dutchman, whose name I do not know, but is quite insignificant."

Smokey began to pace with small steps, but he kept to his side of the upturned drum.

"I won't bore you with every detail. I'm sure you're both quite capable of finding the story on the wonderful world wide web for yourselves. But legend has it that the diamonds were stolen by an Englishman who wanted to present them to Queen Victoria as a gift. But during his passage back, his ship sank and he drowned. As luck would have it for our sparkling little friends there, the captain of the ship took them and climbed aboard a lifeboat with two other men. They floated around at the whim and mercy of the ocean for weeks. Then they eventually washed up in Portugal. From there, they made their way to France and found the British Army, with whom they planned to travel back to England."

"Not much of a story, Smokey," said Rupert.

"But there's more, my boy," said Smokey. "You see, they couldn't decide on who carried the diamonds, seeing as none of them trusted each another, so they took turns in carrying one each. Eventually, one night, when all around them was silent and stars filled the black sky, one of them stole the pair."

"He stole off his mates?"

"That he did, Rupert, that he did, and God did strike him down, you see. The other two woke just as he was leaving and found the diamonds missing. They were both overcome by some kind of godly power. No longer in control of their own senses, they tore the third man to shreds with their bare hands."

"So then there was two," said Rupert.

"That there was, Rupert, that there was," replied Smokey. "From that point on, and to this very day, the diamonds have never been in the same pair of hands. When the two regained their composure and realised what they'd done, they were shamed and went their separate ways. The first diamond stayed with the man's family for years, hidden and deemed too dark to reveal to the public, as if it were possessed by some kind of demon."

"And the second?" asked Rupert.

"The second, my boy, was given to Doctor Hans Sloane, who in case you didn't know, was the man that founded the Natural History Museum from his very own collection of natural wonders from around the world. It was a collection worth a small fortune in its own right."

The brothers took in the story in silence.

"And that," continued Smokey, "if I'm not very much mistaken, is the very diamond that sits before us, reunited with its demon twin brother for the first time in nearly two hundred years."

Smokey stopped pacing and faced the twins.

"Fascinating, isn't it?" he said with a jovial tone.

"Yeah, fascinating," said Charlie. "So can we take them now?"

Just as he spoke the words, a crash of thunder ripped through the night and seemed to shake the old building. The skylight high above them smashed, sending hundred-year-old shattered glass raining down on the men, along with the body of Glasgow George, which landed with a sickening crunch of breaking bones beside the upturned oil drum.

Standing in the rain outside the factory, on the canal towpath and in the shadow of a willow tree, Harvey took in the scene.

On the far side of the canal, the south side, residential apartments stood new and clean. Lit windows with open curtains showed families or bachelors closing their days off with TV or dinner. Two women ran from a building to a waiting taxi, laughing, and drove away to somewhere more glamorous.

On the north side of the canal where Harvey stood, the scene was far bleaker. Old factories stood in a line. Once, they might have loaded canal barges with their produce, or taken deliveries of coal that may have floated down from further north.

The buildings were all derelict, and it was only a matter of time before a wealthy investor tore them down to mirror the south side. The buildings were all dark save for one, in which the tall arched windows glowed liked fiery orange eyes cast from the fires inside.

A van was parked outside on the narrow lane, and an old chain link fence ran the perimeter of the factory. It was the only security for the property.

Harvey stood and watched.

He'd seen two men enter the building through the single door he himself had used before. The two men had been identical and were the exact two men he was looking for. But the absence of other people tugged at Harvey's mind. Men like the brothers rarely came to a meeting alone.

An iron bench had been placed on the towpath for walkers to rest. Beside it was a waste bin. Harvey checked inside and found what he was looking for, an empty glass brandy bottle. Someone who had sheltered in a nearby factory probably left it. Harvey fetched it out and returned to the tree.

He waited a full minute before he moved again.

Nothing stirred except the trees and the perpetual rain.

A huge crack of thunder and immediate lightning carved a hole in the sky and lit the factory in three successive flashes.

Outlined against the old brickwork, Harvey saw the shape of a man beside the door. He was stood with his hands in his jacket pockets, a sign that he was either over-confident or ill-trained.

The full minute finished. Harvey stepped forward and launched the bottle high in the air. It came down and smashed on the ground twenty yards to the man's right.

As planned, the goon heard the shattering glass and went to investigate. He was a wide man, stocky but short. The way he walked gave Harvey the impression that he was mostly muscle and trained heavily.

Harvey stepped out from the trees and walked slowly across to the factory. He fell into the shadows just as the man looked around, confused as to who had thrown the bottle.

Harvey worked his way behind the man, taking small, slow

steps. The rain covered the sound of his boots, but Harvey could still hear the man's heavy breathing like grunts from some docile beast.

The man stopped. He seemed to sniff the air.

Harvey slowly pulled his knife from the sheath inside his leather biker jacket.

"I hoped you'd come," said the man without turning.

Harvey froze.

The man turned to face him.

"They said you would, and you did," he continued. Then his eyes caught the shiny blade in Harvey's hand. The man gave a laugh then stopped. "It is *you*, isn't it?"

He'd been waiting for Harvey.

"That depends on who it is you think *I* am," replied Harvey. Raindrops were now dripping from his brow.

"You're the one that killed my mates," said the man. "You're Harvey."

Harvey didn't reply.

"Let's settle this like real men. Put that away, son." He gestured at Harvey's knife.

"You first."

The man grinned and reached inside his jacket. He pulled out a handgun, black and slick with the rain.

He threw it to one side.

Harvey let the knife fall from his grip. The weighted blade found the soft mud and stuck in, leaving just the carved handle sticking out of the ground.

"They were two of the toughest men I ever met," said the man. "You must be pretty tasty."

Harvey didn't reply.

In an instant, the man charged at him. Harvey braced his feet and swung an uppercut to the oncoming man's face. It connected but had no effect. Instead, the full weight of the charging man collided with Harvey, taking him off his feet and onto the ground.

Before Harvey could react, punches rained down on his face. His arms were pinned by the man's knees, and they rocked from side to side with the hammer of each blow.

The man reached back to get his full weight behind one last final blow, but Harvey twisted, raised his leg, and hooked the punching arm. Using the momentum, Harvey pulled the man off with his leg and reversed positions before landing his forehead into the man's nose.

Harvey landed three bone-crunching head butts before he was thrown off. Both men rolled away from each other, each wiping rain and their own blood from their eyes. With three confident paces, the man came again at Harvey. His left hand was cocked to defend his face, while he held his right ready to deliver a jab.

Harvey raised his own hands, but the jab smashed through his block and into his throat. Harvey gasped for air as his crushed windpipe recovered. But more punches came through. A shot landed on Harvey's left side, and immediately, a right hook connected with his face.

Harvey went down.

"Come on, boy," said the man. "I thought you were tough."

Harvey dragged himself away, putting distance between them.

"Get up," the man shouted.

Harvey pulled himself to his feet and stood just as the man collided with him again. Harvey landed on his face only to receive a succession of rapid punches to his kidneys. He tried to suck in air, but only managed to cough up blood, thick warm and metallic.

Suddenly, Harvey was hoisted into the air like a rag doll. The man held him high above his head, took three steps, and tossed him into the factory wall beneath one of the arched windows.

"This is easy," he said. "There's no way you killed Mad Bob."

Harvey rolled onto his back and saw the man walking away. He was working himself up, breathing heavily.

Then Harvey saw his chance. A maintenance ladder fixed to the side of the factory wall was a few feet away. Harvey pulled himself to his feet, using the wall to balance, and slid along the old bricks to the first iron rung. He clung to it as if his life depended on it. Then he took a glance behind.

The man had seen him.

"Where do you think you're going, boy?" he said, and charged at Harvey once more.

Harvey dug deep. He jumped up and grabbed the highest rung he could reach. The iron was slippery with rain and sharp with years of rust. His kidneys screamed in protest, but he pulled his body clear of the man, who slammed into the wall beneath.

Harvey's feet found the rungs and he began to climb. Each pull of his arms to the next rung tore into his beaten body. His head swam from the blows, and more than once, he swung to one side as his mind tried to regulate his balance.

Harvey cleared his throat and spat blood down at the man, who was slowly catching up. Just when he thought the ladder might go on indefinitely, Harvey fell forward onto the huge, shiny and slippery pitched roof.

Dragging himself clear, Harvey rolled onto his back and clambered backwards to the apex. The big man lumbered over the crest of the ladder a few seconds later, grinning.

"Is this it, is it?" he asked. "You want to be thrown from the roof?"

Thunder rumbled closer and the rain felt heavier.

Harvey pushed himself to his feet once more and stood. He

was taller than the man who followed him. But the height advantage was nothing compared to the lightning-fast jabs that came at him. Harvey dodged, bending right and left, his eyes planted on the man's.

But the punches kept coming. There was no room for Harvey to return a blow. Then suddenly, the man stopped.

He was catching his breath.

Harvey had been waiting for the moment. He lunged out with a straight kick to the man's chest. It connected and sent him stumbling backwards, but not down.

Instead, he returned with a vengeance, swinging wild punches at Harvey's head, chest and stomach. Most missed, but a few destroyed Harvey's attempts at blocking and connected.

The last blow stopped Harvey dead.

The man stepped in close, reached up and put his fat fingers around Harvey's throat.

He squeezed.

In an instant, tiny lights swam in Harvey's eyes. His breathing grew thin, like sucking air through a tiny straw.

The man grinned up at him.

Harvey reached up, groping for the man's face, until he found his eyes and jammed his thumbs into the sockets.

His throat was released, and Harvey fell to the wet, tiled rooftop. He slid down and dug his boots in, just managing to stop himself from sliding to the edge.

He looked up at the man who was now several meters away and bent double clutching his face. For the first time in the fight, Harvey charged. Just as a rumble of thunder built somewhere far above, Harvey gathered his strength, took a deep breath and ran with everything he had up the pitch of the roof.

His full weight slammed into the man's legs. Jamming his shoulder into the man's mass, Harvey lifted him, barely off the roof tiles. But it was enough. Harvey carried on pushing with his legs. He roared as he called upon all his strength. As the man toppled forward and Harvey's momentum began to falter, the two men fell together.

Harvey slammed into the rooftop with his arms wrapped around the man's legs. The sky split with an enormous crash of thunder and a flash of lightning that seemed to light the entire world.

Suddenly, the man's full weight dragged Harvey fully up the roof and he glanced up, expressing a split second's realisation that it was over. Just moments before Harvey too fell through the hole, he let go.

There was no scream, no thud of a body hitting the floor. From where Harvey lay, there was only an empty expanse of wet and shiny rooftop with a smashed skylight, pouring rain and a grumbling sky.

CHAPTER THIRTY-EIGHT

The two brothers jumped back in surprise, but Rupert noted the lack of reaction from Smokey. He pulled his handgun from the inside of his suit jacket.

"What the hell was that, Smokey?"

Smokey peered at Glasgow's twisted and smashed body.

"He's one of yours I think," replied Smokey.

Charlie pulled his gun. Both brothers held their weapons aimed at Smokey, who seemed unperturbed.

"That's fucking Glasgow George, Smokey," said Rupert.

"Ah, George," said Smokey. He returned his gaze to Rupert. "Shame. But you really should be careful where you point those things. They can be lethal, you know?"

"Smokey, we're going to take the diamonds and we're going to leave," said Rupert. "Who do you have up there?"

"I have friends in many places, Rupert. But on the roof of this here factory?" He shook his head. "None that I am aware of."

Rupert stepped forward and reached out for the diamonds, but Smokey pulled back one side of his coat and lifted the gleaming double barrels of a shotgun.

"Do yourself a favour, my boy," he said. "Step away from the diamonds."

"Smokey," said Rupert, "what are you doing? There's two of us and one of you."

"There is indeed two of you," said Smokey. "But I have two barrels, each with a nice red cartridge in, and you know what, boys?"

"What, Smokey? This is not going to end well for you, mate."

"Before I loaded my shotgun, I took a marker pen, a black one. On one cartridge, I wrote the letter R. Tell me, Charlie, what letter do you think I wrote on the other one?"

Charlie fixed Smokey's questioning gaze with his own hateful stare. "C?" he replied.

"C," said Smokey. "That's right. Well done. But the only problem is I cannot for the life of me remember who is on the right..." He returned his stare to Rupert. "And who is on the left."

An awkward silence hung as the brothers tried to fathom Smokey's smug grin.

"I hope you don't mind sharing?" asked Smokey.

"There's no need for this, Smokey," said Rupert.

"On the contrary. You see, those diamonds are a legacy. There's history in them than runs deeper than you can imagine, and well, I just couldn't live with myself if I let you two clowns walk off with them."

"What do you care about history?" said Rupert. "I told you we'd give you a cut."

"Oh you did, you did, my boy. But tell me Rupert, do I look like I need a cut? My house is so big there's rooms I don't even know about. When I make a cash withdrawal, Rupert, the fucking bank manager comes to my house in an armed security van. It is true that I admire and respect what you two pair of degenerate ponces have done for yourselves with your bars, clubs and with the help of Neanderthals such as our late friend Mr Glasgow George here. But you are not ready to wield the responsibility that comes with protecting the beauty and grace of rare and expensive gems such as the Demonios Gemelos."

"I'm not going to bear the responsibility of anything, Smokey," said Rupert. "I'm going to sell them and sit on a beach-"

"With semi-naked women," said Charlie.

"Oh, is that right?" said Smokey. "Oh, well in that case, I'm afraid the answer is irrefutably no. I can't allow these to be sold. Who knows what hands they might fall into? They'd be gone forever, boys."

Rupert gave a little laugh. "*You* don't get to allow the *Bond* Brothers to do *anything*, Smokey. We're *taking* the diamonds, and we can either do that with you standing there, or we can do it with you laying down there, with George, and with a bloody great hole through you."

Rupert took another step towards the diamonds.

"And if we're giving speeches, I suggest you listen hard. Our families go way back. We've always been allies and on account of that, I'd sooner not have to kill you. But if it means the difference between walking away with those two diamonds or not, I *will* kill you, Smokey."

Rupert aimed the gun at Smokey's head.

"So, Smokey," Rupert continued. "The ball is in your court, I believe. What's it going to be?"

Smokey remained completely still with his shotgun aimed from his hip at Rupert. "I told you I have two barrels on this shotgun, didn't I?"

"You did, Smokey. But my patience is running out I'm afraid."

In a flash, Rupert lowered his weapon and pulled the trigger, sending a round through Smokey's knee. Smokey went down. He hit the hard concrete floor with a slap. His shotgun discharged harmlessly into the roof above. Rupert stood over him and watched him writhe on the floor, growling through gritted teeth.

"Dad," a voice yelled from the shadows behind Smokey. A female voice.

Rupert swung his weapon into the shadows.

"Who's there?" he called out.

Smokey continued to laugh.

"I said who's there?"

"Have you met my daughter?" asked Smokey.

"Your what?" said Rupert.

"My daughter, Rupert. I don't believe you've had the pleasure. Lola, would you care to join us by the fire?" he called. Smokey winced at the pain that was shooting through his leg.

"Lola?" said Rupert. "You must be mistaken, Smokey. Lola's enjoying a nice slow death as we speak." He grinned at the man on the floor.

But his grin turned to confusion as Lola LaRoux stepped from the shadows.

Rupert's head suddenly dizzied.

"You can't be..."

Smokey laughed. "You lose, Rupert. You got the wrong girl."

"Regardless," said Rupert, "you're down there and I'm up here. The diamonds are mine."

"No, Rupert, wrong again. The diamond *belongs* to me. It always has. The man that carried it from France-"

"Your ancestor?" said Rupert, as the pieces fell into place.

"It was stolen many years ago from my father, and we've been searching for it ever since. So when you and your greedy brother stole it from us, you woke a very old and angry beast, Rupert."

Smokey laughed hard, then grimaced at the pain in his leg.

"And then you gave it back to me to look after, you schmuck. But I'll give you credit for the plan. It would have been good had you done your research."

"You played me?" said Rupert.

"You always *were* the smarter of the two. But I suggest you use those brains and stop pointing that gun at my dear Lola. I'm quite the protective father, Rupert."

"Charlie," said Rupert, seeing the upper hand shift, "take the diamonds."

But Charlie gave no response.

"Charlie?" said Rupert. "I said take the diamonds."

Rupert glanced around to find an empty space where Charlie had been standing.

"Charlie?" he called.

No answer came.

Smokey laughed through his pain.

"Where is he, you bastard?" said Rupert.

Smokey continued to laugh.

"I said where is he, Smokey? You could have lived. Don't make me do this."

Smokey stared up at him, smiling.

"Put the gun down, Rupert," said Lola. She stepped into the fire light pointing her own handgun at Rupert.

Rupert aimed back at her, but the move gave Smokey a chance to shift his heavy shotgun from his position on the floor. He aimed it directly at Rupert.

"Now, Rupert," he said. "I believe that *we* have two guns, and *you* only have one."

"Rupert," called Charlie from the shadows behind.

"Charlie? Where are you?"

No response came at first. Then a weak and frightened voice replied to Rupert. "I'm here, by the wall."

"What are you doing? Come here," said Rupert.

"Rupert, help."

Rupert looked down at Smokey, who just smiled back.

"We find ourselves in a very tricky position, don't we?" said Smokey.

"Rupert, help," called Charlie.

"I'm coming, bro," said Rupert. "What's wrong?"

Rupert backed away, switching his weapon from Smokey to Lola and back again. He passed the diamonds, collecting them both with one hand, and stuffed them into his jacket pocket.

"I wouldn't do that if I were you, Rupert," said Smokey.

"Rupert, help."

"I'm coming," called Rupert. "Why not?" he said to Smokey. "You don't honestly believe in a curse?" Rupert continued walking backwards. "Charlie, where are you?" he called.

"I'm here," replied Charlie. His voice was weak and raised an octave.

Rupert turned to find a dark wall in front of him, swathed in shadows.

"Charlie?" he whispered, suddenly aware of a presence around him.

As if on cue, thunder boomed, followed a few seconds later by two flashes of lightning. It was then that Rupert's eyes fell on the sight of his beloved twin brother hanging from the wall with two meat hooks protruding from his chest.

"Charlie?" whispered Rupert, and ran to his brother across the soaked concrete floor.

Grabbing him by his waist, Rupert tried to lift Charlie off the hooks, but he was too heavy and Rupert's handmade leather soled brogues slipped on the wet floor.

"Who did this?" he yelled at his brother, as if it was his fault.

Charlie just stared back at him as if he'd accepted death. Pity filled his eyes and his wordless mouth hung open.

"Charlie?" said Rupert.

"Drop the gun, Rupert," said a voice, new, but familiar, with a tone of exhaustion.

Rupert span to find Smokey being supported on one side by Lola, and on the other, a man who held a burning length of wood picked from one of the oils drums.

"I told you I had two barrels, Rupert, didn't I?" said Smokey.

"Get him down," Rupert shouted, his voice thick with tears.

"The diamonds, Rupert," Harvey replied.

"The diamonds?" said Rupert. "Why don't you come and get them."

Rupert stuffed his free hand into his pocket and pulled out the two diamonds. They glittered in the fierce fire light, alive with the power of the flames.

"Take them off me," Rupert spat.

The man simply smiled back at Rupert as if it was the answer he'd been expecting. Then he let his hand fall forward and tossed the burning lumber into the pool of liquid in which Rupert stood.

Immediately, the pool took light. A rush of excited blue flames tore across the room, sucking in the cool air with a hiss.

Rupert cried out in shock as the flames engulfed him. Instinct told him to run, but brotherly love held him on the spot. He reached for Charlie, throwing both arms around him. He pulled and pushed, trying to lift his brother high off the hooks, but the flames licked at Rupert's hands and soon engulfed them both. Charlie's suit and skin simply fell away at his touch. As the flames reached his face, Rupert screamed as every inch of his body was seared and the sickly odour of burning flesh filled his mouth and nose.

Charlie's face seemed to look down at him, retorted in silent agony as the flames too licked at his face. Rupert clung desperately to his brother's waist. But as the fire took hold and the pain overcame any strength Rupert still had, he slid down to Charlie's knees and lay in the pool of burning petrol with his arms wrapped tightly around his brother's legs.

Through the heat haze and his burning eyes, Rupert faintly caught movement. Smokey had lifted the shotgun from beneath his coat. He seemed to watch Rupert's suffering for a few seconds longer until finally, he pulled the trigger.

CHAPTER THIRTY-NINE

By the time she and Reg ran through the single doorway of the factory, Melody knew they were too late. Three figures stood beside the wall to her left, standing over the remains of a smoking and smouldering fire.

A thick, sickly odour filled the huge space.

The man in the centre turned his head to face them as they approached and the girl readied her weapon.

"It's okay," said Harvey.

Melody stepped up to the trio.

Harvey held his hand out to relax the man he and the woman were supporting. "They're after me," he said.

"I get the feeling we're late to the party," said Melody.

"Smokey, Lola," said Harvey, "meet Melody Mills and Reg Tenant."

"Ah, I've read about you, Miss Mills," said Smokey. "It's a pleasure. I'd love to stay and chat, but as you can see..." He gestured at his ruined leg.

"You look like you're in need of medical attention, sir," said Melody.

"Medical attention and a stiff drink, miss," replied Smokey. "It's been a long night."

"And these two?" said Melody. She nodded at the charred remains of the Bond Brothers.

"They won't be much trouble any longer, Miss Mills," said Smokey.

"And you must be Lola?" said Melody. "The brothers had quite the plan for you and your friend Fingers."

"You're police?" asked Smokey.

"Sir, can I ask you to drop the gun?" said Melody.

"Oh, indeed, Miss Mills." Smokey span the shotgun around and he offered it to Melody butt first. "Would you mind taking it? But please be careful. It's a Purdy, very old and extremely expensive."

Melody took the weapon from him.

"One of a pair you know," he added. "Quite apt really, given the circumstances."

"Harvey?" said Melody, as she broke the shotgun, checked it was empty, and hung it from her arm. "What are we going to do here? Someone has to pay for this and the diamonds."

"Is that right?" replied Harvey. He passed Smokey's weight onto Lola and made sure she was steady. Then he stepped forward, bent down to Rupert's blackened and still smoking bones, and snapped back his charred fingers to reveal a pair of perfectly unscathed, flawless, 200-carat diamonds. They were identical in appearance and weight.

Harvey removed them from Rupert's hand, which crumbled to ash as Harvey stood up.

The diamonds, lying cupped in Harvey's hand, sparkled even in the dim light of the factory. Holding them high, Harvey peered through them to catch the dim light from the arched windows.

"Incredible," he muttered.

"They're absolutely beautiful," said Lola.

All five of them were silenced by the almost magical glistening, until Harvey lowered his hand and closed his fist on the two rocks.

He turned to face Melody and the others.

"As I see it, Melody," said Harvey, "the brothers had themselves an accident."

He stepped past the bewildered Lola and Smokey and held out an upturned hand.

Melody held her own hand out, palm facing up, and felt the weight of a single half of the Demonios Gemelos as Harvey released it.

For the smallest fraction of time, he held Melody's gaze. The slightest of smiles appeared on his face then faded to Harvey's standard non-emotional gaze.

As Melody began to speak, Harvey turned away.

"But what about the other-" she started.

"I believe this belongs to you," interrupted Harvey, addressing Smokey. He dropped the twin diamond in the palm of the old Jewish man.

Smokey's hand closed around the diamond without even a cursory glance then disappeared into his pocket.

"Toda," he said.

Harvey raised an eyebrow.

"It means thank you in Hebrew."

Harvey nodded.

"But wait, what about *Fingers?*" said Lola, suddenly panicked. "Did the brothers get him?"

"No," said Harvey. "I got him."

His remark was met with an intake of breath from the group.

"It's okay. I let him go. I told him to get on the first flight he could," said Harvey.

"It's a shame I didn't listen then, wasn't it?" said a voice from behind Melody. "I could be somewhere much warmer by now."

"Fingers," cried Lola. She held onto her father but held an arm out for Fingers to join her.

He gave Lola a hug and shook her father's hand. Then he ran his eyes over Melody and Reg before letting them fall on Harvey.

He gave a small nod of thanks.

Harvey returned it.

"Well," said Smokey, "I'd love to stay and chat. But I'm afraid I'm slowly bleeding to death here. So if you'll excuse me."

Fingers left Lola's side and picked up the side that Harvey had previously supported. The three slowly made their way past Melody and Reg, but before they reached the door, Smokey stopped. He turned and with a voice of authority, wisdom and gratitude, addressed them all.

"Before I forget my manners," he began. "I can't begin to tell you how grateful I am. And the rest of my family too."

Harvey, Melody and Reg all nodded at him.

"I'm sure my father and the generations of Abrams before him are all up there somewhere smiling down that our diamond is back home."

He let the comment hang in the stale air, and smiled.

"You'll be hearing from me," he said. Then with the help of his daughter and her friend, he left the factory.

CHAPTER FORTY

Just two days had passed since the incident at the factory. There was a lot for Harvey to take in but not much for him to do.

He took one final look at the single Demonios Gemelos diamond, sitting prettily on its cushion in the Natural History Museum. A flock of tourists had gathered around to see the now-famous diamond after its recent theft and return.

The tourists closed in and Harvey stepped away, taking the fastest route out of the building and ignoring the strange looks from passers-by who stared at his bruised and swollen face.

He shouldered his backpack, pulled the visor down on his helmet, and rode out of London for good.

His senses felt numbed to the people, places, and cars he passed. But it felt good to be back on his bike and heading back to his little farmhouse in France.

He just had one more stop to make before pointing his bike at Dover and opening up the throttle.

Harvey regretted leaving before he had a chance to talk to Melody, and to Reg. He missed his old friend a little. Melody had tried to talk to him in the factory, but it hadn't been the time or the place. He'd walked away, leaving Melody standing there for the second time in his life.

Part of him regretted walking away. He knew she was good for him. But the beast inside him was volatile, and he knew it. He couldn't bring her down with him.

Thirty minutes later, and around thirty miles west of Guildford, he clicked the left-hand indicator on, slowed the bike into second gear, and rode between two huge wrought iron gates, which he estimated at about thirty feet tall.

Before him was a long gravel driveway, which swooped around past an enormous lake. A series of smaller fountains sprayed water at the foot of a central fountain. The lake was awash with frothing white water.

Past the lakes and the fountains stood a huge grand house, at least three stories tall, with balconied windows and an entrance that even the Royal Family would be happy to walk up.

He parked the bike at the foot of the eight long curved steps, removed his helmet and peered up at the two huge double doors.

A man in a tuxedo and white gloves stood waiting between the balustrades for Harvey to climb the steps.

"Mr Stone?" he asked, as Harvey approached.

Harvey nodded.

"This way, sir," the man replied, and walked briskly to the house.

The huge front doors closed behind Harvey.

"Follow me, if you will, sir," said the man.

Harvey followed once more and allowed himself to be led through a pair of ornate doors of dark wood, past huge oil paintings in frames that looked as expensive as the paintings themselves, and along a corridor so long, Harvey couldn't even count the doors that led from it.

At the far end of the corridor was one final set of double doors, of matching dark wood and intricate mouldings.

Harvey stepped through and was surprised at the sudden change in surroundings. The doors opened out into a huge glass conservatory with brilliant white window frames. The natural light in the room was overwhelming in contrast to the grandeur of the house Harvey had just walked through.

Ahead of Harvey stood two doors that opened out into an immaculate garden filled with manicured hedges and flowers that exploded in colour, contrasting the thick greenery they bordered.

To Harvey's right was a table surrounded by chairs and holding raised plates offering fruits, nuts, and small pastries. A silver tray with coffee completed the scene, containing a small display of china cups, saucers and silver spoons.

But the biggest surprise was to Harvey's left. A large, white-framed bed stood encased in a flowing net curtain.

In the bed, sitting up and beaming at Harvey with grateful admiration was Smokey the Jew. He was dressed in white pyjamas, with his braided payot swinging freely beside his face and a dark skullcap perched atop his head.

"Mr Stone," said Smokey, "I'm so pleased you made it. Won't you join me?"

"How's the knee?" said Harvey as he stepped up to the foot of the bed, noticing for the first time that Smokey's half of the Demonios Gemelos sat in a rich purple cushion on his side table.

"I won't be walking unaided again," replied Smokey. "They removed my leg below the knee. But I'm breathing, and my heart is strong." He followed Harvey's gaze and smiled gratefully.

Harvey nodded.

"Good," he said. "I'm glad to hear that you're feeling okay."

"You look like you've been in the wars yourself, Harvey," said Reg.

"I'll heal," replied Harvey. "I always seem to."

"Well," began Smokey, "without further ado, I'd like to offer you my sincere appreciation for helping my family regain its long lost property."

"It's okay, Smokey," said Harvey. "I don't need your money."

"My money?" said Smokey with distaste. "I'm not offering you money, my friend."

He swept a smile across the room, as if checking they were alone, and then rested his eyes on Harvey's.

"I have a proposition for you."

Harvey didn't reply.

The End.

STONE DEEP - SAMPLE
STONE DEEP - BOOK NINE- CHAPTER ONE.

The Defeat of the Floating Batteries at Gibraltar commanded the grand, opulent gallery. Even to Cordero Diaz, whose knowledge of the fine arts could be written long-hand on the rear of a cigarette packet.

The painting was more than just a picture painted on a canvass. The brush strokes, visible in the texture of the oils had purpose. They weren't simply the result of applying colour to the creation using a brush as a medium, the strokes conveyed tones, shadows, and direction, and complimented neighboring colours, tones and shadows. The depth of the foreground, with it's hues of greens, and deep shadow were not there to fill a gap between the background and the content, the foreground had lines that drew the viewers eye to the life of the art; its very heart and soul. The soldiers on horseback, described in so much detail that a modern photograph could not portray the scene with more clarity. Finally the washed, blend of pastel colours used to invoke a terrifying scene of battle, anguish and carnage, invoked the smell of gunpowder, fire smoke, and ultimately, death.

The painting was a masterpiece.

At nearly eight metres by six metres, removing it from its position of glory some five metres high on the wall of the gallery would require planning, but it was not impossible. If it was possible for one man to create such a masterpiece, it would be possible for a team of men to steal it.

Falling in with a guide and a host of tourists, Cordero played the part of an inquisitive visitor well; this wasn't his first rodeo. He knew the rules of engagement. Invisibility was key.

The remainder of the tour, although interesting, was spent examining security. The Guildhall Gallery in the City of London was not protected by lasers. A web of infra-red beams were not switched on when the doors were locked, ready to sound the alarms should an inexperienced intruder fall foul of their purpose.

Cordero noted the camera positions, and with a series of timely nods from one of the planted guards who had been working the gallery for several weeks, Cordero was able to snap the security challenges they might face under the guise of artistic interest.

"Erm, excuse me," said the guide, as Cordero leaned over the barrier to photograph a Monet in the corner of the room, directly below a security camera, "there is no photography allowed. Did you see the signs?"

Cordero stepped back from the painting.

"Yo no entiendo. Lo siento," he replied.

"No esta permitido," said the guide.

"Ah," said Cordero, feigning a sudden understanding, "Ci, lo siente." He finished with an embarrassed smile as the eyes of the tourists all returned to the guide, who continued to explain how the gallery was destroyed by German bombers during the blitz of World War Two, and how many of the paintings that were displayed, were removed and sent for safe keeping just three weeks before the gallery was hit. Cordero ignored the speech, fully aware of the galleries history; instead he memorised the brand of security camera, a detail that the photo would have captured and allowed the tech guys to plan the security breach.

The tour took another forty minutes to complete, during which Cordero noted several paintings that would be far easier to remove and steal, and were likely worth a great deal more, black market or not. But Hector had specified The Defeat of the Floating Batteries at Gibraltar, claiming it to be lifetime ambition to own the masterpiece, and as a result of his dream, the logistics of the operation were minor details. And if Cordero knew Hector as well as he thought he did, it would not be long before the painting was installed in Hector's house, although he couldn't think where it would go, for a painting of such magnitude would require a room with walls far greater in size and grandeur than Hector possessed.

As the guide completed the tour, and answered the final question from an Asian tourist, Cordero loitered for the opportunity to thank the guide in his best broken English, and to apologize for his lack of thought stating that he was overcome with admiration for the painting.

"It happens every day," smiled the guide, "I hope you enjoyed the tour?"

"Ah ci," said Cordero, in an attempt to sound enthused, "perfecto," he finished.

The guide opened the door to the staff only room, and offered Cordero a "Ciao," as he stepped away.

Cordero took a final glance up the sweeping staircase into the gallery, catching a final glimpse of the target, then turned to leave.

The walk from the gallery to Liverpool Street train station took just five minutes, and the train to the leafy London suburb of Brentwood was sat waiting at platform eight.

Cordero chose an empty carriage, although three schoolgirls who seemed to be skipping school joined him and sat noisily a few seats away, laughing at nothing, while playing music through one of their phone's loudspeaker. They girls disembarked at Stratford Station, where a man entered, and selected a seat at the far end of the carriage.

Cordero searched through the images he'd managed to get before the guide had caught him taking photos, and he sent them to Diego as instructed. Diego would ensure the images were shared with the rest of the team, and by the time he arrived back at the garage, plans would already be in motion.

As the train approached Brentwood, Cordero stood and waited by the doors. The man at the far end of the carriage, a slight man who was engrossed in his phone ignored him. A lady at the other end of the carriage, who Cordero had not noticed, collected her bag and stood beside the doors closest to her. She checked her watch, and seemed to be peering out of the window, perhaps checking for her husband who would be collecting her. Or maybe it was a lover? Cordero could smell her perfume, it was rich, not floral, but light, with a hint of sandalwood and fruit. She un-fastened the top button of her blouse. Cordero smiled to himself and pictured her steamy clandestine meeting with her infatuate. Perhaps she would allow her hands to wander as he drove them to his house. Perhaps she would offer a glimpse of whatever lie beneath the small skirt she wore; a tease he thought, before the delights of their taboo relationship reached the security of his home.

Cordero followed the woman from the train, down the concrete steps and through the barriers which were left open during the day, until rush hour. He slowed his walk, and admired the view of her behind, hoping to catch a glimpse of whatever lucky man would be sharing the next few hours with her. The station was empty, the street outside appeared quiet.

The woman turned left. Cordero followed.

She walked thirty metres from the station entrance, then with a practised casual manner she glanced back once, then slipped into the passenger side of a waiting SUV. Cordero slowed, then stopped and made to cross the road. He turned his head to check for traffic as the first blow connected with his throat, crushing his windpipe. With wide panicked eyes he span to face the attacker, but found nobody.

Cordero gasped for air, he leaned on a post to support himself, then from nowhere his chest felt like it had been hit with a hammer and the static sound of a tazer rang like a warning bell as fifty-thousand volts raced through his body, stunning his senses. The tazer stopped and Cordero reeled from the blast of energy as a thick bag was pulled over his head. Cordero fought to remove it, he lashed out at the attacker but a hard blow to his gut sucked the wind from him; a second blow, which slammed into his temple rocked his vision and turned his world from a dizzied array of spinning lights to the peaceful, pitch dark of unconsciousness.

Also by J.D. Weston

Award-winning author and creator of Harvey Stone and Frankie Black, J.D.Weston was born in London, England, and after more than a decade in the Middle East, now enjoys a tranquil life in Lincolnshire with his wife.

The Harvey Stone series is the prequel series set ten years before The Stone Cold Thriller series.

With more than twenty novels to J.D. Weston's name, the Harvey Stone series is the result of many years of storytelling, and is his finest work to date. You can find more about J.D. Weston at www.jdweston.com.

Turn the page to see his other books.

THE HARVEY STONE SERIES

Free Novella

The game is death. The winners takes all...

See www.jdweston.com for details.

The Silent Man

To find the killer, he must lose his mind...

See www.jdweston.com for details.

The Spider's Web

To catch the killer, he must become the fly...

See www.jdweston.com for details.

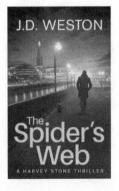

The Mercy Kill

To light the way, he must burn his past...

See www.jdweston.com for details.

The Savage Few

Coming 2021

Join the J.D. Weston Reader Group to stay up to date on new releases, receive discounts, and get three free eBooks.

See www.jdweston.com for details.

THE STONE COLD THRILLER SERIES

The Stone Cold Thriller Series

Stone Cold

Stone Fury

Stone Fall

Stone Rage

Stone Free

Stone Rush

Stone Game

Stone Raid

Stone Deep

Stone Fist

Stone Army

Stone Face

The Stone Cold Box Sets

Boxset One

Boxset Two

Boxset Three

Boxset Four

Visit www.jdweston.com for details.

THE FRANKIE BLACK FILES

The Frankie Black Files

Torn in Two

Her Only Hope

Black Blood

The Frankie Black Files Boxset

Visit www.jdweston.com for details.

FREE EBOOKS FOR YOU...

As a gesture of thanks for buying this book, I'd like to invite you to the J.D. Weston Reader Group. Members of my reader group benefit from:

- A free eBook.
- Freebies as and when I run them.
- News of discounts from my author friends. (there's usually one or two of them running a promo at any given time).

Visit *www.jdweston.com* for details.

A NOTE FROM THE AUTHOR

West London is way out of Harvey's comfort zone, and being mixed up in a diamond heist, well we all know that's not his thing. But there was something about this story that kept digging at me. Harvey isn't always in his comfort zone, such is life, but I wanted to convey that Harvey is Harvey wherever he is, whatever the situation, he'll rise to the top.

There's a cyclical element to Stone Raid that I loved. The twins, the diamonds and the mystery, and while a part of our minds is processing the romance behind the story of the diamonds, no amount of history or legends will stop Harvey wading in and dragging everything back to reality kicking and screaming.

The Natural History Museum is an incredible place to visit. If ever I'm looking for inspiration, I can be sure I'll find something there.

There are stories tucked into every hidden nook and ancient cranny of London, and Harvey's next adventure is no different. If you thought Stone Raid was a wild ride, you'd better make yourself comfortable and find something to hold onto because Stone Deep is the most action-packed Stone Cold Thriller yet.

I hope you continue on, because Harvey is far from done yet.

Thank you for reading.

J.D.Weston

To learn more about J.D.Weston
www.jdweston.com
john@jdweston.com

ACKNOWLEDGMENTS

Authors are often portrayed as having very lonely work lives. There breeds a stereotypical image of reclusive authors talking only to their cat or dog and their editor, and living off cereal and brandy.

I beg to differ.

There is absolutely no way on the planet that this book could have been created to the standard it is without the help and support of Erica Bawden, Paul Weston, Danny Maguire, and Heather Draper. All of whom offered vital feedback during various drafts and supported me while I locked myself away and spoke to my imaginary dog, ate cereal and drank brandy.

The book was painstakingly edited by Ceri Savage, who continues to sit with me on Skype every week as we flesh out the series, and also throws in some amazing ideas.

To those named above, I am truly grateful.

J.D.Weston.